DEAN HAMID

LOVIN' SAFARI

DEAN HAMID

DEAN HAMID

ACKNOWLEDGMENTS

I would like to thank my God, and all praises are due to him. I dedicate my success to my parents, Minnie & AC. Thanks for being supportive of me in a painful, dark situation. My mother is always saying, '*Baby…we family*!' I miss you, and I love you, both.

Thanks to my sister, Sharon for your continued struggle to keep the family together and for being supportive in this endeavor. Writa'z BLOC forever, sis!

My daughter, Courtney for saying the one word that I needed to hear when I needed to hear it. *Focus*! DeVante stay strong and let what you're going through be a lesson, and a blessing! Thank you, Deb, for raising strong children in my absence. May God continue to bless you, I love you.

Thank you, Dean Hamid Presents family for your support, love, nurture, and craft. For giving me the strength, and the opportunity.

My homeboys, and homegirls: Jay Scott, Curtis Thomas, Mark Hendrickson, Barry Jones, Mike Macky Alford, Darleen Oxendine. Greg Gee Richardson, Riko, Benee Nee Holiday, Bibi, Maurice Lott, Antoinette Griffin, Sam Smalls, Drew Bey, Florzel Thompson, Bobby Bilal Cherry, David Tony Stephens, Jacqueline Williams, Brandi, and Rhonda Stephens.

My Uncle Camp…this man deserves his own line! Thanks, Unc!

Thank you to my extended family, and fellow authors for their support: Tina at I Am Tina Louise Graphics, Polow Don, Carlos Torres, Tee Blocker, Mick & Ra, Gerrold, Now Born-Wild Life Publishing, Randy Coxton, Wahida Clark,

DEAN HAMID

Nuance Art, Zel Owens, Dutch Harlem, Tight Rope, Book Chick Monica, Jade Green, Saja Jay, Tiffany Lawson, Arthur Brice, Kia Storm, Tammy Capri, UBAWA, Toastmasters Club #58, Conan Himes, Friday, and trust me, a whole host of others. *My love and respect*!

LOVIN' SAFARI

PROLOGUE

The moon peeked its head inside the cool, pastel-green colored room illuminating its light on the face of the gentleman that sat in the powder blue, easy-chair watching the stars party as they twinkled. As he gazed off from the moonlight, he turned towards the door behind him and his mind transfixed back to reality.

He crossed his legs and pulled up his pants slightly, then nodded. The small ankle strapped Kimber .32 automatic still remained snug. As he listened closely, he could hear his heartbeat rise and fall off his ribcage, against the shoulder holster and Ruger .9mm.

He turned in his chair now more from boredom than anything else and checked his surroundings once more. The thirty-five-hundred-foot condo he was in was exquisitely decked out, with expensive oak and marble furnishings. Large ceilings and a winding marble stairway twisted its way upstairs towards the bedrooms. The place where he would hopefully end up if the evening played itself out right.

His ears twitched, and this time, he turned fully, facing the bathroom where the walk-in shower was. He could hear the tiny streams of water massaging her body and intermingling with the midnight chirps of crickets pouring in through the window.

He sat…he waited…it wouldn't be long before she'd come out. He'd play his role as a gentleman and help to dry her off, then hopefully be escorted upstairs to the room where he would make the passionate love, he now fantasized about with her.

As he pondered, he also thought about the task at hand. Was he up to it? It was a job…a job that paid well, he reasoned bitterly. He sighed, then turned back around and leaned back into the chair.

"How did I get to this point?" he asked himself.

CHAPTER 1

Summer 2000: St. Louis, Missouri

The loud bell rang, and kids poured out of the chipped brick, tatteredly painted and cracked walls of a school. It was their last day and they showed their gratitude by hauling ass like freed slaves. Textbooks were strewn across the grass as they scattered in all directions. Except for two young boys who sat off to the side, on the steps watching it all and discussing their plans for the summer.

"So, Zeus, what you got planned, bruh?" Marcus asked.

"Don't know for sure." Zeus stretched his long, lanky legs out and looked off. "Wouldn't mind going somewhere…out of town."

"What!" Marcus stood up. "And leave good old St. Louis and go where?" he laughed.

Zeus got up and playfully shoved him. "I know, right?"

They walked off the school grounds to a whole different atmosphere. A different school, school of hard knocks, with damn sure no books. St. Louis may have been home to the Cardinals, but it was far from the element of freedom that the logo portrayed. Zeus and Marcus lived right in the thick of it, Fountain Park.

"Damn…there goes those knuckleheads." Marcus kept his eyes peeled on the group of older boys in front of him as they watched him and Zeus come down the block.

"Fuck them…" Zeus said. "They ain't really built like that. There's just more of them than us."

"Yeah, and their people belong to Gunzz's gang," Marcus emphasized.

"Yeah well, fuck him, too."

Marcus moved closer to Zeus, he admired his buddy. He wasn't the biggest cat in the world but by far the most fearless. They were close as all hell, and if anything went down, they'd be in it together. Then talk shit about it later, that's the way they rocked. The boys in front of them stood up and blocked the sidewalk.

One of them, a dude named Zak, stepped forward. "Where the fuck y'all lil' niggas think y'all going?"

Marcus just looked at him. Hell, he was no bigger than they were. But, like Zeus said, there was just more of them. They never really did no real damage, just fronted like they would. They'd get a couple of quarters from them and then let it go. Go buy loose cigarettes and call it a day. But today, they didn't have nothing, and they were borderline junkies. Their addiction was now dependent on him and Zeus. They were shit outta luck tho'.

"Yo' man…we ain't got shit for y'all niggas today," Zeus said back to him.

"What?" Zak turned toward his boys, that were about four deep. "You heard this little muthafucka? He ain't got shit for us!"

Zeus dug deep into his pants and pulled his pockets inside out. "See."

Zak looked, then turned towards Marcus. "How about you?"

Marcus didn't move, he was scared, then he finally slid behind Zeus. He had a couple of dollars. The money he'd save for a down payment for a pair of Jordan's he'd eyeballed at Dick's Sporting Goods.

He whispered to Zeus. "I was going to lay-a-way those kicks today."

'*Damn*,' Zeus thought.

Marcus had saved faithfully for that. He talked religiously about those damn sneakers. He wasn't going to give them shit. They'd have to take it in blood and when he gave him that look Marcus knew that that was the deal.

"Naw…he ain't got shit either."

Zak was no slow leak, he'd already spotted the bulge in Marcus' pants and he'd already committed to the next level. Which was to take it from him. He, or at least they needed that little piece of change. They were past the cigarette stage now and wanted a nickel bag or two of that good dog-food their boss Gunzz had.

They stared each other down. Zeus and Marcus already had their fists balled up. Zak and his boys moved in towards them. It was going down, and they stood firm. Zak moved in first and was about to raise his hand.

"Hey…what the fuck is going on!" Zeus and Marcus turned their heads across the street and grinned.

Zak and his boys frowned as they stepped back. "Nothing man!" Zak spat.

It was Vervin, Zeus' uncle, and right now their savior. He came over to where they were and stepped in between them. "Yo', man, what's up, everything cool?"

He turned and looked at Zak and them. They backed off. Zeus looked at him, he knew his uncle didn't like them, and he also knew Unc had enough in him to whip Zak's ass and his boys wouldn't do shit.

Zeus just nodded his head. "Naw, Unc…everything cool." He and Marcus walked past them with his uncle by their side.

Zak snarled at him as Marcus looked back. Somehow, he knew this was far from over.

"Look, Zeus, them guys putting the tim on you or what? You want me to handle that…talk to Gunzz?"

"Naw, Unc, seriously, we cool!"

Marcus caught the front end of the city bus going downtown as it turned the corner. "Yo', I gotta go. I better go ahead and put this money on those sneakers…while I can."

Zeus dapped him. "Hell yeah, you do that. I'll catch up with you later."

Zeus and his uncle watched as Marcus got on the bus going to Dicks. Zeus' uncle was an old-g around the neighborhood. He'd already done two bids for bodies up the road and was well established as a gangster, nothing to fuck with. Since Zeus' father caught that elbow in '99, he was also now his father figure and Zeus' moms didn't mind.

He was the oldest and she had three children already to keep up with. Her brother stayed with them when he wasn't *out of town.* He'd given her the money to keep the roof over their heads and food on the table. She was okay with Zeus spending time with him. She just wasn't good with how her brother made his money. But, Vervin didn't give a fuck.

"Uncle Vervin, you leaving out tonight?"

His uncle nodded. "Don't worry about that, lil' bruh. Just do the right thing and stay your ass out of trouble."

Zeus nodded. "Yeah…stay out of trouble."

"You don't need no record."

They'd had this discussion already because Zeus showed interest in what Unc did. Least from what he told him so far. Unc didn't mind, but he had to show him the right way. Sure, there was college, and all that, but growing up in Fountain

Park, inner city, ghetto St. Louis; college wasn't much of an option. Zeus showed no interest in the gangs and that was a plus. The only real friend he had was Marcus, and they stuck together through thick and thin. Hell, Vervin thought, why not show these little dudes the business? He intricated the business of killing, the business of being a ghetto assassin.

****

The time came and went, and Zeus grew into a young man. His uncle took him on outings teaching him things like how to shoot, load, and strip down a weapon. How to case his mark. That meant spending a lot of hours watching and following people without them knowing. A.k.a, stalking, and of course, the biggest one, how to drive.

He asked his uncle why not just roll up and murk them. His uncle explained to him that real bad boys move in silence. No heat meant more Jobs meant more money. Zeus and Marcus were his prodigys now, but Unc still made them attend school and read and learn. The more they knew and were educated, the closer they would fit in. Zeus asked him why he himself still stayed in the hood? He made enough money to move somewhere better.

He explained to them that right now the hood meant protection and assured that he didn't stand out. More and more Marcus and Zeus proved their loyalty. But they still had one thing they needed to do, together. They finally kicked Zak's ass. They beat him up so bad he ended up in the hospital. They beat him with a bag full of quarters. Vervin frowned on that. He was paid a visit by Gunzz as a result. Vervin told him it was just a bully issue, and to pull his boys back. Gunzz agreed, he didn't want any problems either. After all, he knew he would need Vervin's services again in the near future.

As time progressed, Vervin's calls started getting slower and less frequent. The mobsters started using younger men who were bolder and had a steadier aim. While Vervin was sniffing dime bags of dog food, listening to jazz music and nodding off. These young men were putting in that work, trying to leave their mark. One day, Vervin had gotten a call that he really couldn't afford to miss and still maintain credibility. When Zeus searched for him, he was later found held up in a dope den, high as hell. Zeus informed him about the call and after some coaxing he finally persuaded Vervin to explain the job to him. Zeus knew Vervin was in no type of shape to do it, so he figured he'd handle it himself and show-off his capabilities.

He called on Marcus for help, but Marcus had other engagements, so he pressed forward. He went to his uncle's stash and picked out a Sig Sauer .45 with two extra clips, and a silencer for the job. He used the address he'd gotten from his uncle and when he arrived at the house, no one was there. He did the research like his uncle had shown him and found out his target had a gallery. Zeus arrived downtown St. Louis at the posh place and waited patiently while stalking his prey.

Finally, after a few hours, the man stepped out with a young girl in tow. She couldn't have been much older than Zeus. So, he had to be the mark. He couldn't afford to wait for the time to be right again and decided to get it over with. He slid the clip in and around into the chamber, then screwed the gas charged silencer on the muzzle. He reached into his pocket, pulled out a skull cap and slipped it over his face, then took a deep breath.

"This is it!" he said to himself.

As the man came out, he turned the corner into an alleyway, where he had a car parked. Zeus had to get at him before he made it there, not knowing what he had inside. So, he crept up the block across the street and crossed over coming up behind them. He turned the corner and the man had his back turned away from him. He pushed him up against the car and spun him around. The man's eyes bulged wide, but it was more from surprise than fright.

"I told them, I'd get the money!" he yelled and stepped in front of the girl, putting up a defensive stance.

Then he glanced into the car. Zeus knew it was more than likely, that he had a gun. Zeus couldn't let him go for it, so he reached for his gun and started to aim. But the long legs of his assailant kicked at it and connected causing the gun to hit the ground. Zeus only had two choices at that moment. Either go for his gun or stop his target from going for his in the car. Zeus jumped on his back and started punching his face.

His keys dropped to the ground, followed by Zeus and the man and they started wrestling. Then the man reached into his coat and pulled out a stiletto. Zeus jumped to his feet and glanced at his gun. Zeus started for it, but he swung the blade and caught Zeus on his right cheek. Blood gushed profusely out of the wound and ran down his neck, but he still managed to dive on the gun. Before he could use it the man also dived on the gun and on Zeus. Once again, they wrestled and finally, he had Zeus on his back.

He raised the blade up high and aimed to plunge it into Zeus' chest. Zeus finally reached the gun, and at the same moment, he swung the knife down. Zeus managed to roll to the side and get a hold of his bearings, then he aimed and fired. He caught him in the chest. The man looked down at the bullet hole, then at Zeus, and still tried to lunge, but it was useless.

He fell over, then looked up at the girl. "Run!" Those were the last words out of his mouth.

Zeus' nerves were frayed, but he had to pull himself together. His skull cap was bloody, so he took it off. He got up off the ground staggering against the car. The girl just stood there in shock. He looked over at her. She had light brown eyes, chocolate brown skin, and long, black, silky hair that dropped past her shoulders. Her lips were full, and they quivered in fear. When she stared back at Zeus, there was something about her that drew him into her.

However, this was business and she was a witness. He pointed the gun at her, and she bent over crying. He got closer to her and put the muzzle up to her head. She looked up at him. This was the part that his uncle never prepared him for. Killing a person while they looked you dead in your eyes. Especially when those eyes were from the most beautiful person he'd ever seen in his life. He backed up slowly, staggering, raised the gun in the air and shot out a window.

"Get the fuck outta here…now!" he hollered at her.

She stood up slowly, still staring in his face, the slash on his cheek and eased past him. Then, she turned the corner and hauled ass up the street. Zeus looked down at the man and kicked him to make sure he was dead. Then stuffed the gun into his jacket and eased to the corner of the building. It was dusk and not too many people were out, but he had to haul ass too. He didn't know if the girl was going to the cops or not. He eyeballed the route he came, knowing he couldn't get on the bus like he'd done earlier.

DEAN HAMID

He ran opposite the Mississippi River towards Tucker Boulevard making his way to Kings Highway Boulevard, back to Fountain Park. He looked back only once after that to make sure the distance between him and downtown St. Louis got wider. When Zeus finally made it home, he went into the house and made his way to the basement. He pulled on the hinges, lifted the trap door and made his way down to his uncle's stash spot. After wiping the gun down, he meticulously put it back into place. He figured he'd come back later, strip it down and clean it. Right now, he had blood all over him and had to clean up before somebody saw him…*especially his mother.*

He slowly made his way back upstairs and crept into the bathroom. He stripped down and jumped into the shower. As he stood under the steaming hot water, he let it calm his nerves. But when he raised his head towards the showerhead the cut stung like all hell once the water got into it. He held onto the shower curtain to keep from buckling. Once he got out, he wiped the mirror dry and looked at his face. His cheek had been sliced open, but not all the way through. He was thankful for that, but it was definitely going to need stitches.

He pulled out some gauze and applied it to his face holding it with his hand. He was going to have to find Marcus and come up with a plan to get stitches from somewhere. Most likely from a ghetto doctor, then come up with a lie to tell his mother. He opened the door and standing in front of him was his, Uncle Vervin. He scanned his face, reached for his hand bringing the gauze down, and shook his head.

"What the fuck did you do!" Uncle Vervin asked.

Zeus pushed past him into his room. "I took care of the business!"

"The business? What the hell…"

"Your ass was too high to do the job. And…you…we… needed the money." Zeus' voice trailed. "Thought you wouldn't mind."

His uncle sighed and walked over to him. "I wouldn't mind, huh?" He reached into his pocket and pulled out some cigarettes. "Well, I'll tell you this…" He pulled out a smoke, put it up to his lips and slowly pulled out a light. Once he lit it, he blew the smoke into the air and faced Zeus. He shook his head, then backhanded him sending Zeus to the floor hard.

"What the fuck was that for?" Zeus asked getting up off the floor, holding his face.

"You, stupid motherfucker…your fast ass!" Vervin fussed.

"What! No one saw me."

"You're probably right, but…" He was just about to smack him again, then he stopped. "You killed the wrong person…we won't get paid!"

"What…what do you mean?"

"The mark was the girl!"

Zeus' head spun when he heard that. He'd let her get away. All he did was murder a man.

"You see. That's the part of the business you have to learn…" His uncle turned and walked to the door. "Patience…but, you paid for it."

He turned back around and pointed to his cheek. "With a mark, you'll never forget. Now get dressed so I can take you to the doctor. And then…explain this shit to, Gunzz."

"Why?"

"Because the motherfucka you killed owed him money."

CHAPTER 2

Present Day

Safari stared at her velvety chocolate skin and frowned as it laid over a large mole sitting slightly above her left eyebrow. When she was younger, her mother, Gladys would swoop her thick, long, black hair into a ponytail that hung lazily against the back of her neck. Safari would cringe as it exposed what others called a beauty mark. Safari didn't feel the same way though. When she was in school the kids would laugh and tease, saying she had a *booger* on her forehead.

The only person who didn't partake of such teasing was her best friend, Rainey who was comfortable being invisible. Rainey wasn't ugly, but her beady eyes, pug nose and wiry, russet hair compliments of her Caucasian mother and African American father meant she was different. Safari embraced being different down to her name given to her by parents who loved *Wildlife*. From the day she was born until her mother's tragic automobile accident at the age of five, they'd take her to St. Louis' Zoo every Saturday. It was a family ritual that usually ended with a scoop of ice cream on a hard cone.

While she missed her mother, she also grieved her father who was murdered fifteen years earlier. To this day, she'd never uttered a word to a soul about what happened to him. Instead, she was diagnosed with selective mutism for months fearing that she'd never get to avenge her father's murder had she whispered what occurred that night.

Without hesitation, Rainey's parents took her in, instantly bonding them for life as sisters instead of just best friends. Safari was now what others called an orphan. This helped her further learn how to develop a tough skin. She wasn't much of a fighter but what she lacked in brawn, she made up for in brains.

Because of her love for insects and animals, payback came in unusual ways. Safari laughed to herself thinking about the time she and Rainey collected red fire ants in a jar, one day for Juke: the school's bully. Juke really had it in for them. It was mostly because unlike the rest of the girls, they ignored him. They twisted off the jar's cap and placed it underneath his seat in the cafeteria. Good old Juke jumped up screaming and hollering like he'd caught the Holy Ghost. Even though no one could prove it, he knew they were behind it. After that day he fearfully stayed out of their way. Especially, Safari who made it her business to wink at him each time they saw each other.

Safari looked in the mirror and sighed studying her soft, toasty brown eyes. Her mole was now covered by her full, freshly permed hair and threatening to peek out. She huffed, swiftly swooping a large bang of hair behind her ear. It created a fullness that complimented her doe eyes and round face. She poked out her full lips, then wiggled them around before she dabbed on a shimmery lip gloss.

"It's almost time," said Rainey, sticking her head into Safari's room.

After graduation, they both went on to attend and graduate from Harris-Stowe State University. It was Rainey's informal rites of passage to confirm her black roots and Safari's way of remaining close to home. Well close to the cemetery where both of her parents rested. Rainey secured a

BA in Urban Ecology while Rainey graduated at the top of their class with a degree in Mathematics.

Safari sucked her teeth, flashing a fake smile at the image many called beautiful. She hated this part about *dating*, the part where you pretend to care or was some weak woman looking for someone to save her. Truthfully, Safari stopped being weak once she became parentless.

Her hard heart was shielded by a voluptuous body most men wanted to taste and have their way with. This one guy, the one waiting for her, however, was different because it wasn't about a date. It was a business meeting. The problem was the more she made it about a meeting, the more Rainey wanted to make it about a date. She had no time for dating, but after great persistence from Rainey and her waiting suitor, she agreed hoping she wouldn't regret it.

"I know, Rainey," she sighed with a smirk. "Now no staying up, I have my key."

"Well, too bad, I need details!"

"How do I look?" Safari asked standing up with a slow turn.

Just like her room that was complete with an exquisite large, Victorian, Queen-size bed, a dresser and cosmetic area that sat across from a body-sized mirror, Safari did everything with class and on a large scale. Her cream-colored slacks hugged her firm thighs and waist, outlining her hour-glass shaped figure. Her coral, crisscrossed off the shoulder top showcased her breasts, that were so perfectly melon shaped that even women were in awe. Most called it, DNA but Safari called it her secret weapon. Her toes were freshly painted and glittery like the lip gloss lacing her lips.

Once she stopped and looked at Rainey, she froze. "What…something wrong?"

She looked at the mirror trying to see if something was on her back, smoothing down her slacks that flowed down in a wide-legged fashion. Her fragrance lingered in the air. It was vanilla and pear, a fragrance she'd mixed herself. Mixing perfume was a small hobby that had morphed out of a class project in college.

"Amazing," Rainey said more to herself admiring Safari's firm derriere.

"Rainey!"

"What? I'm serious, you are!" She chewed her lip smiling. "I just wish you would do this more."

"Do what more?" Safari huffed. "This is not a date, remember? It's just a meeting. Isn't he a friend of, Marcus' anyway with his corny ass?"

"Whatever, Safari, and yes he is. He's a very important man. One who can get us the money we need for our none profit organization. Can you imagine all the youth that are less fortunate? You know like…well…"

Safari shook her head giving Rainey the side eye. She never looked at herself as being less fortunate. Truthfully after her parents died, she was left with a hefty life insurance policy that remained in a trust fund until she completed college. Somehow, she received a letter her freshman year from social services. Instead of spending it, she tied it up into various investments called imports and exports. Investments that only she knew about and wanted to keep that way.

"Well, like what?" she challenged crossing her arms.

Safari could see Rainey shrinking as her beady eyes looked everywhere but directly at Safari. Safari loved Rainey but there were times she wondered where they stood. In school, she'd catch guys looking at her only for Rainey to come home and say they asked her out or gave her their number. Then once they went off to college, any guy that seemed remotely interested in her, somehow ended up in bed with Rainey after a drunken, sex-filled night in their dorm room.

"Nothing, Safari," she sighed. "I sent you because you have this way with men. Shoot, they fall all over you and you don't even have to try!"

"That's because I don't. I have better things to do with my time and *my* body," she said, with a smirk.

"You mean like saving yourself," she huffed, rolling her eyes. "I swear if I had what you were working with, we wouldn't need this meeting."

"*And we don't.* I'm doing this for you because I believe in it. I also know we could do some great things right here in St. Louis with these kids. I mean don't you remember how broken our desks were or how tethered our textbooks were in school? And let's not talk about the park…the crime-ridden park where we could barely swing because the chains were always broken?"

"Yes, I was there…I remember," she replied softly chewing her lip. "Well, Mr. Black's commencement speech last week went viral. His view of strengthening the economy in communities that look like him was impressive and powerful. Not to mention, he's one of the largest donors for HBCUs. I can see us now being the recipient of his benevolent spirit."

"Well, are you his agent trying to land him a Nobel peace prize? Or are you making sure I'm good enough to land a date after tonight? Anyway, he's old enough to be our father. Even if I were interested, I certainly wouldn't be dating anyone his age."

"He's not! I checked," she slipped and said.

"You checked what?" Safari really was not into dating and hearing how this meeting was starting to sound like a date bothered her.

"He's like in his late forties, maybe early fifties. Damn, Safari, lighten up."

"If I wanted to date my granddaddy, I would. I want nothing from, Mr. Black besides a partnership, Rainey. *A business partnership* to be exact. The more I think about it, it's a joint venture. You should come."

"No…no…no," she replied with her face turning red. "I mean look at me. My hair is all over my head and my wardrobe is nothing but tights and tanks. Come on, Safari."

"Not true, you clean up well," she said grabbing her by the chin giving her an air kiss.

"Yea, only when you dress me."

It was true. While Safari could put a basic outfit together out of jeans, a business jacket, and a camisole. Rainey didn't care to bother unless she had to. It was one of those things her ex Jamal would fuss about if they had a councilmen event or Gala. While Safari was a true fashionista, on a Friday night she enjoyed curling up with a book, a glass of wine and her loyal, vibrating bullet. That's when she was being simply herself and not the side Rainey knew nothing about.

"Look, Rainey. We have one shot and one shot only to see what he wants to do and that's tonight. What if I stumble and give him incorrect stats? I mean math is your thing," she whined.

"You won't and if you do, just text me. See," she said holding up her cell. "This will be glued to my hand until you get back."

"But then when will I have time? You know I am in the midst of a very important project at work that will be taking up a lot of my time. Then I have a few meetings lined up with the president and the Alumni affairs that will require more travel."

"There you are being so…so…"

Crossing her arms, Safari waited, hoping that Rainey's brain caught up with her mouth. She was not about to explain herself to anyone let alone her best friend who barely gave who she slept with a second thought.

"So, what?"

"Skeptical, suspicious, always looking and waiting for the worst in everyone."

"Well, that's because I'm right most of the time. If you would just listen to me more, I'd be living alone. And you'd be in marital bliss with, Jamal."

"Fuck, Jamal," she snapped. "And you're right, just call it off. I can do this my damn self another time."

Safari felt a pang of guilt coursing through her body. It wasn't Rainey's fault that she didn't get close to people. It was like anyone she tried to love was taken away from her. Well, anyone except Rainey and here they were in the mid-twenties still living together.

"No, you won't. Look, I'm sorry," she sighed, approaching Rainey for a hug. "I just think we can get the money another way. I mean the way you keep pushing me on the man. I'd swear he's expecting a date, so let's hope that Mr. Black keeps it professional. Then we can have a girl's day tomorrow just for good ole' time's sake."

Rainey's eyes lit up. No matter how much they appeared to bicker, she loved Safari. She was the sister she never had and now business partner if this deal with Mr. Black went through. Then she could brag to Marcus a guy she was secretly dating, how she pulled it off since he coined Safari as bougie the day they met, at probate when the Deltas was revealing their new line. Safari was a member of the prestigious Delta Sigma Theta Sorority, while Rainey specialized in other things. Things that resulted in her drunk in bed with the likes of Marcus. At first, she wanted more, but now, she was all in for the real prize that would soon be revealed.

Besides she had no time for love after her failed engagement to, Jamal her ex-fiancé. Who is now one of the City Councilmen. Instead of going to work and working, he was working his secretary who was now his wife and mother of his two children. Once Jamal played her like a two-dollar bill, Rainey was now out for self.

"Fuck love," she said to herself.

It was all about the Benjamin's, a side of her Safari was none the wiser. It was funny how they knew each other so well but were strangers at the same time.

CHAPTER 3

The blue hazed smoke hovered high above the air in the room like a cloud against the large framed, tinted window overlooking downtown St. Louis. In the background the arches of the St. Louis monument lingered precariously setting the mood as the man who smoked on the fat Cohiba leaned back looking out at them. He was deep in thought as his mind pondered heavy on the meeting he had planned. His name was Gunzz Black, the biggest mobster in St. Louis. Most people remembered him back when he was just a two-bit nickel and dime thug doing extortion in the hood. Now, thanks to his connections he'd established out of Chicago, he was now, *the man*. Although it took a while for him to climb the mountain top, it wasn't without casualty.

Not wanting to get his own hands dirty, he hired hit men to do his dirty work and to kill off his competition. After going through his fair share, he settled with his best two: Zeus and Marcus. Both were well trained by Vervin, Zeus' uncle, so he could depend on them for results. Zeus was the best by far, and most organized. He didn't take no shortcuts, but his buddy Marcus could be compromised. That's why he had to keep an eye on him.

He kicked his feet down off the windowsill and turned towards his desk. Sitting in front of him was Marcus. He nodded his way, then got up and walked toward the sofa where he sat.

"So, you think, he'll do it?" He leaned over and eyeballed him directly.

He was always trying to intimidate him, but it never worked. Even though he was tall, standing at six-feet, he was still rather light in comparison to Marcus. He weighed only one-hundred and sixty-five pounds to Marcus' one-hundred and ninety pounds. He rubbed his ear: it was his habit. Ever since the shootout that took half of it off by a rival gang that rolled on him at a gym. He escaped that one, but he sought revenge in the way of a hit. Marcus did the job for him, and he was successful.

Ever since then he always looked to him for advice when he felt threatened, and this imminent hit was one of those moments. As far as the gym incident, he told him simply, *"Don't play no more ball."*

"Yeah, …he's the best. What're your worries?"

"It's been a while now, I figured he would have taken care of it already."

Marcus turned his way. "I told you he'd do it. You just can't do a job like that real quick, it has to be subtle." He leaned forward. "Well planned!"

Gunzz walked back over to his desk. "Hell, for the money I paid…"

"Look, Gunzz, he'll do it alright."

Marcus leaned back deep in thought. He was sure Zeus would take the girl out, but exactly when that would be was out of his control. Gunzz was right, it had been a while. Maybe, he should have done the job himself, but with Rainey and him being so close, it would look too suspicious. The set-up was already made anyway. Zeus didn't have a clue as to who the girl was, but Marcus would have never thought he'd have fallen for her, too. Granted, Safari was fine as all hell, but Zeus was the type that showed no emotion…no love.

This girl here had him twisted already. Maybe, it was part of his plan, but Marcus doubted that, though.

He got up and said to Gunzz, "Look, I'll get up with you later, I gotta make a run." He had to go see Rainey and find out what was going on with the broad.

"Hey, Marcus!" Gunzz hollered out. "If he doesn't do it…you will, right? After all, you recommended him."

"Yeah, yeah." Marcus reached for the door and opened it, then turned and looked back.

He knew what that meant, he'd have to kill Zeus, too. He was hoping it wouldn't have to go that far, but if it did, oh well. He walked out of the office building to his car. His swag had the women who worked there staring because he had sex appeal. Marcus was smooth at six-one and the well built, athletic type. He worked out on a regular basis, both him and Zeus. But he knew what separated them in the ladies man department. His curled hair, light skin, and bright brown eyes. They went for it, but still in comparison to Zeus' tall, mysterious, demeanor, and more muscular physique he was still the interior. That made him jealous, and at the same time envious of Zeus. But Zeus was his homeboy, his partner, his friend. It was Zeus who'd put him in the assassin game when Vervin offered it to them.

Marcus was in awe of everything about Vervin. From his calculating hits down to his skill-set, but Vervin saved the best for his nephew Zeus. Then Zeus would share with Marcus what he wanted him to know, which was mostly crumbs. Marcus had to figure out a lot of things on his own and he didn't like that. He kinda knew it wasn't intentional on Zeus' part. Zeus liked him and didn't want him to be hurt or killed. Zeus felt Marcus had a legitimate future that was better than his.

Marcus was smart, he'd even gone to college and that's where he'd met Rainey and Safari. After getting to know each other, he learned of Safari's background. In no time, he put two and two together and confronted, Gunzz who confirmed she was the girl he wanted killed back in the day. The girl that his homeboy Zeus let get away that day when he killed her father. She would also become the girl that inherited her father's business, then paid off all his gambling debts, and on the urgings of her, BFF Rainey continued the business of importing and exporting. It consisted of paintings, exotic furs, and animals, as well as money laundering. Lots of the money belonged to Gunzz.

Now Rainey's greedy ass wanted to cut her BFF out of the picture, so she and Marcus could take over. So, now they needed to get Safari out of the way, permanently. Marcus took out his keys when he spotted his Jag and stopped, then surveyed it, and the area. It was his nature to scan the vehicle for any unknown or foreign objects, mainly a bomb. Once he confirmed that it was clear, he hopped in and started it up. Then he reached into his glove compartment and pulled out his phone. He searched through a few texts, mostly from women, then pulled up his contacts and pressed: *Rainey!*

CHAPTER 4

"Shit," Safari muttered getting stuck at the light.

She wanted to be the first to arrive but her debate with Rainey had put her behind schedule. That was their usual dance, Rainey would compliment Safari. Then Safari would tell her how beautiful she was or could be. Rainey would deny she had any potential, then snap at Safari for just being smart and beautiful. Safari looked in the mirror and poked out her pouty lips before rubbing them together to even out the gold shimmer in her lip gloss. She dabbed the top of her lip which sweated occasionally when she was frustrated or nervous.

"Get yourself together, Safari! You are a damn millionaire. If you can manage priceless, exotic items from all over the world, surely you can handle the likes of a seasoned man who doesn't mind parting with his money," she said carefully swooping her hair behind her ear before the light turned green.

Not wanting to expose what she drove, Safari took an Uber that got her there within twenty minutes. She stepped out and inhaled, smelling the Italian spices that seeped into her nose. She was grateful he'd chosen a Five-Star Restaurant since she already wasn't too fond of meeting him. She gave the concierge her satin wrap and the hostess Mr. Black's name.

"Ah, yes, he's waiting for you," the hostess informed with way too much enthusiasm. "Right this way!"

She could smell the aroma intensifying from the best Italian food in St. Louis. Lucci's was one of the most talked about Italian restaurants in the Midwest. Her eyes danced around the decorum which consisted of Italian, marble floors and crème colored chairs adorning small circulars tables for small and large parties. To her left, she glanced at the large wine rack that carried the best Pinot Grigio and Merlot known to mankind's taste buds. If nothing else, Mr. Black had good taste in food and that was plus.

As they got closer to where he was seated, Safari noticed he wasn't alone. She'd seen him in passing a few times on campus, mostly when he attended charitable events or fundraising dinners. He was smooth, often dressed in a three-piece suit. Tonight, he spared nothing wearing a russet brown suit, with burnt orange alligator shoes. His wavy hair was neatly trimmed as well as the light mustache that gently laid above his rather full top lip he tucked with his teeth.

Safari watched him undress her with his dark, brown eyes that hung lazily at each corner. It gave him a sad look that was until he smiled causing a slight crinkle on each side. As she approached, his smile vanished but his gaze remained steady as they both stood to greet her.

"Safari, sweetheart, I was starting to wonder if we were going to be stood up," Mr. Black said lightly touching her shoulders on each side before he looked at the man he was with.

"Zeus, this is Safari. Safari Kennedy, community activist and alum of Harris-Stowe State University. She studies the uh…community and its inhabitants from an urban perspective. Is that right? Please correct me if I'm wrong."

"That sounds about right," she said as Zeus reached for her hand pulling it to his mouth that was met with a soft kiss.

"Pleasure to meet you, Ms. Kennedy," he almost whispered but was loud enough that his raspy voice tickled her ears.

"Shall we?" Mr. Black asked pulling out a chair. "I took the liberty of ordering a bottle of wine, but if it's not to your liking, order whatever you desire."

"No, this is fine, anything white works for me," she replied, impressed that he'd selected a brand she knew cost him about a thousand dollars.

Zeus studied her body and was immediately stuck on the way her hips swayed from her walk to the way her slacks hugged her curves. Her dark, chocolate skin was flawless, and her long eyelashes were soft almost mesmerizing him. He could even smell the fresh soap and perfume permeating through the air. He was so consumed, Mr. Black cleared his throat to get his attention.

"Oh, you shouldn't have," she replied as he poured her a glass of wine. "It really should be my treat since we requested the meeting."

"If a man allows a woman as fine as you to pay for anything…and I mean *anything*, he's not a man," Mr. Black commented.

He was very handsome for his age. His bald head gave him that seasoned but youthful look. He, too, was dressed in a three-piece suit but his was black, pin-striped completed with black, Italian shoes that easily cost almost a grand.

"Well, I guess I am amongst men."

Zeus watched her full breasts shimmering under the soft light as she and Mr. Black chatted about what she and Rainey wanted to do. He was rather quiet, but his role was simply to be there only speaking to emphasize a point if needed but to ask personal questions here and there hoping she would share more information about herself not already known. Unfortunately, Mr. Black a.k.a Gunzz knew her very well and her father even better. He also knew that Safari was her father's pride and joy.

As the lively banter continued, Zeus even got a rise of what she ordered selecting their linguine. As he sat there, he imagined her spooning the creamy, white pasta against a spoon before dropping it in her mouth against her thick tongue. Then thinking about how her tongue slipped out occasionally licking the sauce from the corner of her mouth had his dick on hard. He didn't want to fuck the target, but she sure was making it hard for him not to.

"So, Zeus," she said, turning her attention to him showing off her pearly white teeth that were so perfect he wondered if they were even real. "What do you think about our proposal? It sort of changes the dynamics of the youth we see dying every day and it puts them in a position to become gainfully employed."

He sat up making sure he was careful with his words. He admired what she had going on. But growing up like he did, he knew most of these kids wanted the life they saw on reality TV or what the hood produced. A bunch of robbing, stealing and getting high. Although he didn't attend college, he was well versed in today's social issues knowing how to turn it on when he needed to.

"Well they say *each one, teach one* and just from sitting here, I've learned a lot," he replied almost lustfully. "Seems like you really understand the psyche of an African-American man or woman exposed to the ills of this world. Some imposed on by generations and generations of poverty. Some simply from poor choices like addiction or as a result of mental health and abuse. You know I have a few young men I mentor. It's nothing formal, but I've had some great success in keeping them off the streets."

"Is that right?" she asked smiling, then taking a sip of wine.

"Yes, Zeus had it tough growing up," Mr. Black interrupted patting him on the back. "I sort of took him under my wing. Early on he started working with me and before I knew it, he was one of my closest business associates, even though I see him as a son."

"So, if you see him like a son, would you consider this a chaperoned meeting we are having with the minors?" she teased wanting to get a rise out of him.

"There's nothing minor about me, Ms. Kennedy… *nothing minor.*"

Mr. Black clinked his glass then raised it in the air requesting a toast. He didn't like the way Safari was controlling the conversation and Zeus. He needed him focused or not involved at all considering how he'd messed up in the past already.

"Here's to a new partnership where we take our community back and take over the world one youth at a time. Here, here," he said with a husky laugh.

"Here, here," Safari agreed lifting her glass to meet theirs.

Zeus gave her a nod followed by a quick wink. He figured it would only be a matter of time before he was able to get her alone and finish the job, he should have fifteen years earlier. Still, his hard dick told him it wouldn't be as easy as he planned as she subtly winked back.

LOVIN' SAFARI

CHAPTER 5

Gunzz sat back watching the pleasant banter between Safari and Zeus and their body movement. He was feeling some sort of way. This meeting was supposed to be special for *him*. His goal was to impress her with his philanthropy and hope she'd become intrigued by him. Maybe, even lean towards another date. He could then kill off the contract on her, then let it go. But that wasn't the case right now. Zeus had already leaned into her. Safari now seemed more focused on him. At least that's how Gunzz was now seeing it.

"So, Safari, Wildlife Corp, your import-export business is doing quite well?" Gunzz asked.

She turned his way only after letting go of Zeus' smile. "Why, yes, it is. In fact, we were thinking about linking up to some world conglomerates."

"Okay…I see! That's excellent, but…you're not on the Board…of Directors, are you?"

"Actually, I am the primary holder…" She picked up her drink and put it to her lips. "But I'm sure you knew that."

Zeus shifted his eyes towards both of them. It seemed like a showdown was ensuing. He wondered, *'where the hell is Gunzz going with this?'* This wasn't part of the plan. He cleared his throat and said, "Hey, uh…I'm going to the men's room." After excusing himself, he got up from the table.

Gunzz was still seemingly in a face-off with Safari. She placed the glass down and said, "Look, Mr. Black, we're alone now. Why don't we drop the facade and put it all on the table? What is it you really want to know?"

Now, she was playing ball in his court. "Direct approach, huh? I thought what was wanted was a donation of sorts for a kid's park, after-school program, or something like that?"

"Well yes, of course…"

"Kids park and programs my fucking ass! Those bastards have been playing on the fucking concrete for years. What's the difference now? Let's get to the real deal! What is it you want?" he spat through gritted teeth.

Safari leaned back. "Excuse me?"

"Remember sweetheart, you called me."

"You know…Mr. Black. I did my homework on you…trust me," she said moving back from the table far enough to cross her long shapely thighs, giving Gunzz a full view. His eyes shifted towards them, then back up in her face like she knew they would. She definitely knew then this wasn't about a donation, at least money wise. "I paid the debt…my father's debt and I don't owe you shit."

Gunzz could only smile, he liked feistiness in a woman. It gave him goosebumps and a rock-hard dick. The waitress came and asked if there was anything else, they wanted. He glanced her way and she raised her wine glass.

"Chardonnay," Safari said.

He pointed to his and replied, "I'll take another Bourbon." Then he turned back towards her. "Your father's debt was indeed paid, but he still owes me."

"Owes you?"

"That business you're sitting on is half mine!"

She smirked. "Half yours! I don't see you or your name on the Board of Directors," she snapped. "You're crazy!" She put the drink down and started to push away from the table. "Or either arrogant as all hell."

"Am I?" he asked leaning forward towards her. "The business was bought and paid for with my money. My dirty money washed clean, courtesy of your old man. Oh, I'm sure he kept records of such transactions…that I'm sure of."

He knew, because of that, he wanted to have her killed. He knew she would be his only heir and transfer his seat on the Board over to her and not him. The waitress came back and put their drinks down on the table.

Gunzz picked his up and took a sip, then continued. "Money that if was traced…could be traced. Money, Ms. Kennedy, that put your smart, black ass in school. I'm sure money that keeps your so-called Board of Directors comfortable. Now listen to me and listen fucking good! I want a cut, a seat on the Board. Perhaps your seat and this can all be resolved." He leaned back and swirled the brown, liquid Hennessy in his hand. "Maybe your kids can even get their fucking playground. And you can be their motherfucking, Mother Teresa, huh?"

Safari stared at him. Actually, studying his seriousness. *'Was this guy for real? Does he know who he's fucking with?'* she thought.

At that moment Zeus came back from the men's room and sat down. "Okay, so what are we eating?"

Safari took a sip from the wine she was drinking, picked up a napkin, dabbed at her lips and tossed it down on the table, then looked at Gunzz. "I don't think I'm hungry anymore." Then she looked over at Zeus. "I'd like to leave."

Puzzled, Zeus looked over at Gunzz with a blank expression. "You heard the lady."

Zeus stood up. "Of course, if it's okay, I can drive you home, Ms. Kennedy." He figured she must have gotten dropped off once her announcement to leave included his presence.

Safari got up and turned towards Zeus, giving Gunzz the full throw of her taut, fat ass, and said, "It's Safari, and of course I'd like that."

Gunzz took another swig and snarled, "Yeah, do that, Zeus." He then called out, "Zeus!"

"Yeah?"

"When you drop her off, stop by my place. We need to talk."

He wanted to let her know who was in control, but Safari knew perfectly who was.

"Oh, I'll make sure he does…" She pulled Zeus seductively by the hand. "I won't have him out…too late."

Gunzz frowned and mumbled under his breath, "Bitch!"

****

Marcus pulled up to Rainey and Safari's apartment, got out, walked up to the door and rang the doorbell.

Rainey quickly opened the door. "Hey, baby!" She opened it wider and Marcus hugged her, then swooped her off her feet and kissed her passionately.

"Wow, what was that for?"

He strolled past her into the living room then over to the bar, that was set up. He picked up a chalice and poured some Bourbon.

"Does there need to be a reason?"

Marcus walked over to the couch, sat down facing her and took a sip. Rainey smiled as he watched her enter the room watching his eyes zoom in on her like she was a luscious, brown piece of candy.

He'd called her earlier, she knew he'd be coming so she dressed for the occasion. She put on tight-fitting jeans that showcased her petite, ample ass and a loose-fitting shirt with no bra, allowing her thick nipples to protrude relentlessly against the fabric. She stood in front of him bow-legged in a pair of five-inch heels.

'If everything goes as planned, she won't be in them too much longer,' Marcus thought.

While she wasn't the fashionista Safari was, she knew what he liked and how to get his attention.

"So, what did you find out for me?" He asked as she sat next to him.

"With Safari?"

"Of course."

"I mean, she has the controlling shares, but she doesn't utilize the vote in any of the business matters. That's handled by the Board. But lately, she has been inquiring about the business arrangements. She definitely wants to dive in feet first."

"Hmmm…I see! So, what about her meeting with, Mr. Black?" He had to see if Rainey knew what was going on because if she knew, Safari did also.

"Mr. Black? Oh, that's just a philanthropy thing. She wants him to donate to a kid's charity."

"How does that fit into our plans?"

"It's just charity work, Marcus."

"No, the meeting."

Rainey leaned back from Marcus a little while contemplating her thoughts then said, "Well…I was thinking about that."

Marcus sat his glass on the table and leaned in towards her. "About what?"

"Me and Safari go a way back, she's like a sister to me. I don't think we actually need to just about cut her throat for her to put us into the business."

Marcus smiled at her ignorance then kissed her neck. "Well, I mean why depend on her…when there's us?" He rubbed her thighs and pushed his body closer on her.

"We could have our own thing." He continued rubbing between her legs and her pussy got wet as hell. "On our own…just us."

He felt her plump titties rise and fall as he continued to rub and play with her now hardened nipple. "But I need you to find out some things for me, baby."

"Okay. I'll try."

Marcus unzipped her pants, slid his hand in between her legs and started massaging her clit. She was moist now, she started grinding against his hand. Marcus slid her pants down, stood up and unloosened his belt, then dropped his pants. His long, eight-inch hard dick sprang out, she quickly grabbed it and slurped it into her mouth and started a slow sensual suck. It got so good, Marcus started pumping even harder into her mouth as he gripped the back of her head. She let up one time to pull off her shirt. Her nipples were standing, and her areola was swollen as all hell. Marcus smiled his approval and started unbuttoning his shirt while she went back to sucking his dick.

He screamed out in pleasure. As he calmed his thoughts, he felt between her legs again and she was dripping wet and hot. He turned her around, bent her over on the couch, then grabbed his swollen dick and played with the pussy, getting it wetter, and wetter until she begged him to put it in.

"You sure because I don't feel like you want it," he teased.

"Yes, Marcus, I do!"

"Tell me!"

"Yes, Marcus, I promise you I do!"

"Do what, huh?"

"Fuck me," she hissed.

"What? I can't hear you!"

"Fuck me, Marcus…fuck me!" she howled not caring who heard her.

Satisfied that he had her where he wanted her, Marcus slid his fattened dick into her pussy, causing her to squirm. He continued to fuck her long and hard until her pussy lathered up. Then he pulled out of her pussy and smeared some of her juices onto her asshole.

"Uunnhhh…Marcus!" she moaned as he stuck his finger in her pussy.

In one swift motion, Marcus fingered her pussy and put the head of his fat dick in her asshole, all at the same time.

"No Marcus…it's gonna hur…" Rainey cried out. Marcus ignored her cries and pushed the head further inside. "Ohhh…Marcus, nooo!" She tightened up trying to stop it, but Marcus reached for her waist and thrust it in, then held his position, causing her to scream out.

"Take it!" he commanded.

"But Marcus, it hurts!" she squealed.

"It doesn't hurt nowhere near as much as you hurt me when you don't do what I ask."

"But I did what you asked," she whined as the pain intensified.

"No, I told your ass to find out everything about the finances that you could, right?"

"I did what I could…"

"I need you to do more!" he declared thrusting harder.

She squirmed and screamed out pleading with him to stop. He spit on his dick and started rough fucking her asshole.

"Naw, I can't! When you do wrong, I gotta punish you."

"Please Marcus…take it out!"

Marcus continued stroking until he could feel the cum at the tip of his dick, then he pulled out and came all over her back and ass. She fell face first on the couch and he laid on top of her and started stroking her hair.

"I don't like to do that, but when you do wrong, I gotta punish you. You understand?" he told her.

"Y…y…yes, Marcus!"

"So, you know what to do now, right?"

"Y…y…yesss, Marcus," she whimpered as the burning sensation from her ass continued.

"Good…real good!" he said as he stroked her hair.

Rainey laid on her stomach and face and sobbed softly into the pillow. She loved Safari, but for what it was worth, she was falling in love with Marcus, too. That or what was even worse, his dick.

CHAPTER 6

Once they were out the door, Zeus quickly gave the valet his ticket while Safari stood quietly almost fuming. He wasn't sure what had happened in his absence, but he was going to use this time alone to get closer to her. He touched her lower back and she winced then wrapped her satin wrap tightly around her arms and chest. The shimmery lotion glowed off her chocolate skin against the moonlight. He bit his lip willing himself to get it together.

"I'm sorry, it's a bad habit," he apologized as he lowered his hand. "You know a man is to supposed to protect and comfort a woman. Seems like you two must have hit a touchy subject back there."

Safari weighed her next words carefully, unsure whether Zeus was none the wiser of her father's history with Gunzz. It's funny how a street mogul in the underground world could be your worst enemy. Or your saving grace depending on your circumstances and how they came into your life. She wasn't sure how he and Zeus were affiliated and until she knew, she decided to play it safe.

"No, not really, he's just…just full of ideas that do not necessarily align themselves with our vision."

"Well, from what I heard, I'm inspired. Growing up how I did, I would have run to any program if the person running it looked half as beautiful as you," he said smiling. "Oh, and let's not forget as intelligent as you are as well."

"See, you were just about to get canceled." She laughed staring at his brown-eyes that crinkled on each side.

"Hey, I'm just trying to ease the tension," he replied. "You know Mr. Black means well, he's tough, but he's solid."

Just then a text came in from Mr. Black.

//: *I saw how you were watching her. Remember, even pretty bitches are still bitches!*

Watching her wandering eye as he read his text, Zeus tucked his cell in his pocket. He was saved as the valet pulled up in his 2017, pearl white, Cadillac Escalade XTS. The windows were midnight dark tinted shielding anyone from seeing inside. Of course, they were illegal, but with half of St. Louis' P.D. on your payroll, getting pulled over was almost impossible.

"This is us," he said ushering her to the passenger door and pulling it open. He reached in about to grab her seat belt before she stopped him.

"Uh, I'm not five," she said as his forehead lightly pressed against her chest. "I think I can handle a seatbelt."

"Sorry," he whispered backing up.

She reached over, grabbed the seat belt and pushed it in until it was secure, then he closed the door.

'I cannot believe she is this got damn fine,' he thought wishing he was taking her home to his bed instead of to her spot.

As he slid in, he leaned over just enough to where their elbows were almost touching. Her thick, dark-skin against the crème colored leather made him pause. It amazed him how the atmosphere, even something as simple as leather morphed into something exquisite and damn near perfect.

"Problem?" she inquired snapping him out of his trance.

"No, none at all. You mind?" he asked, turning on the radio.

"Nope, I already imposed," she softened feeling bad that he was in the middle of her debacle with Gunzz. She wasn't a fool, but she wasn't so sure he was privy to who she really was.

"Don't be! In fact, how about this? Let's finish the night over another bottle of wine, music and whatever your tongue has a taste for."

"My tongue? Do I look like a thot to you, Mr. uh…"

"Beloit…Zeus Beloit

"Oh, you're making love connections or trying to. Let me stop you right there. I'm…"

"Full of shit," he finished huffing as he shook his head.

He knew he was coming on strong but for her to play like she wasn't feeling him was a turnoff. He enjoyed the company of a beautiful woman, but he wasn't about to chase her. He figured he'd stick to his original plan turning the music up loud.

As soon as he did, she reached over and lowered it. "I don't recall telling you where I lived."

"That's because you don't have to, Mr. Black prides himself in knowing who he is doing business with."

"Well, he might but you're just his runner. So, how about you run and tell him his services are no longer needed," she huffed jumping out his truck when he approached the red light.

"Damn!" he huffed, slamming his hand on the steering wheel.

He reached down slipping his cell out of his pocket. He was debating if he should end the night like that and tell Gunzz what happened, or if he should kick it up a notch?

****

LOVIN' SAFARI

Thirty minutes later, Safari barged in their apartment slamming the door, waking Rainey up out of her sex-imposed slumber, after going a second round with Marcus. She clenched her thighs feelings the tenderness between her legs as she rubbed her eyes. Once she got her thoughts together, she realized it was Safari engaged in a heated conversation with herself.

"Ugh, I wish I would stand in the same room as those assholes. I mean who the hell do they think I am?" she spat, then stumped her toe. "Ouch!' she cried out hopping on one foot.

Rainey stood there watching her unsure of what to say. Once Safari got mad there wasn't much anyone could say to calm her down. In fact, once she reached a heightened level of aggravation she was borderline dangerous. Many had never seen that side, except Rainey. She thought back on their freshman year in college, one night when they were coming back from the library. It was finals week and they were there each night almost until the wee hours of the morning.

"I cannot wait until this Physics final is over," Safari complained lugging three textbooks in her arms and a backpack.

"No, you mean this History one. The Physics one is gonna be a breeze," said Rainey almost bent over with an even larger bookbag on her back. "I mean who cares what year the Civil War was when we are at war every day right here in the hood?"

"True but you're only saying that because you're a mathematician and walking scientific genius wrapped into one big ball of hair," she laughed.

"Whatever, Safari. Let's just speed it up, my back is killing me and this big ball of hair will not cooperate."

Safari stopped and sat her textbooks on the ground before neatly tucking Rainey's wiry wild hair back into the bun she'd created on top of her head earlier that day. She wasn't into cutting or curling her hair instead she chose to keep it in a messy ponytail. She smiled as Safari attended to her. It was times like these that she loved having her around. Even when it came to messy ponytails.

"Now, you can look up," she said, pulling the bottom of her chin up. "Let's get out of here since we were the last ones to leave. We should have waited for security, but I need to use the restroom."

As soon as she bent down to pick up her textbooks, a hooded and rather husky guy approached them with a knife in his hand.

"Ahhhh," screamed Rainey while Safari slowly eased her way up meeting the vicious glare he wore.

She could tell he was on something with his dilated pupils and shaky hands. "Shut up, bitch, and give me your wallet!" he hissed quickly looking around.

"Uh…uh…huh," Rainey uttered fumbling through her pocket.

Safari swiftly kicked him in the balls unarming him of his knife. Before he knew what had happened, she'd kicked him twice in the mouth as he tried to get up reaching for her leg.

"Oh, shit!" Rainey cried out as she watched Safari prick the skin on his neck squatting down in his face.

"Listen here you piece of shit. If you think you are entitled to one damn cent of our money because you are flashing a fucking knife that you can't even handle. You're even more delusional than I think you are! Damn, high as a kite crack baby. Now I'm going to give you three seconds to get your pathetic ass up and run. And I mean run or this same damn knife will find its way up your ass."

Rainey felt the chills run up her spine. She knew Safari was tough but even this topped how she handled the kids who teased them growing up. She could see the fiery rage in her eyes that were stretched so wide, they looked as if they were about to pop.

"Okay…okay…okay," the hooded guy pleaded as two teeth hung loosely resulting in a pool of blood on the ground under his chin. "Just don't… hurt me!"

"One… two…"

Before Safari got to three, he was up and running almost tripping over himself as he gripped his tender testicles. Rainey was in shock and almost immovable until Safari stood up and touched her face.

"Hey…hey, look at me," she whispered grabbing her chin yet again. "He's gone! Now let's get out of here before someone sees us."

They gently hugged, Rainey relaxed and nodded her head. If she trusted anyone in the world, it was Safari. She'd watch her time and time again either fight or orchestrate ways to deal with people who tried to take advantage of them.

"Now come on," she said, grabbing her textbooks as she pulled Rainey's hand.

"Hey," she said just barely audible but loud enough to get Safari's attention. "You okay?"

She took her time approaching Safari, who was disrobing right in the living room still talking to herself.

"I mean, I know you're not okay, but… but do you want to talk about it? I can see the meeting may have not uh… gone so well."

"You're damn right it didn't! That…that…uggghhhh! That, Mr. Black, is an asshole. Let's just leave it at that. We don't need his damn support, Rainey. I admit it would be a good look but look at me," she said twirling around in her black, mesh see-through bra and panties. "I could fuck a million out of a CEO over one of the largest banks in the world. We don't need a Mr. Black! Matter a fact, I'll be sure to let the university know that if he ever comes to visit, make sure our paths do not cross!"

"Oh, I'm so sorry," she replied taking a few steps closer.

Safari stopped and stared at her strangely. Something was different about Rainey. It wasn't her hair because it was always unruly and wild. It was the way she walked timidly towards her. Perhaps she could be a tad bit concerned about her outrage but still, something was different. Then she leaned in close to her slowly gazing up and down her neck area. It was red, almost like the shape of fingers.

"Did you eat something that you're allergic to or are those finger bruises around your neck?"

Rainey quickly covered her neck, jumping back. "Um…no!"

"No to what? No, you didn't eat something you're allergic to or no those are not bruises around your neck?"

'*Shit!*' Rainey thought.

She hated lying, especially to Safari who could sniff one out of a rat's ass. She decided to tell her the truth but not all of it.

"Well, you see…I kinda been hooking up with this guy."

"A guy! What guy, Rainey? And in our spot without me knowing?" she asked shaking her head with one of her hands on her hip. "Since when, and I take it you two are pass the *Netflix and chill* phase if his fingers found a home around your neck?"

"Look, relax, I was feeling sorry for myself after you left. I called him up…he answered. I told him I wanted to see him. He knew what that meant, so two adults fucked. Gosh, Safari, stop policing everything I do!" she whined getting upset.

Here she was trying to find out what happened with the meeting and Safari was going in on her about what she did with her pussy.

"Look, thot on, Rainey. Just keep that to a minimum where we lay our head. As for the meeting, don't ask. We will find another donor."

Before Rainey could get her to sit down and talk, an angry Safari snatched her clothes up off the floor and stormed towards her bedroom.

Bam!

After she slammed the door, Rainey reached for her cell and dialed Marcus's number.

CHAPTER 7

Marcus slammed the cell phone down on the table. He was clearly pissed. He'd just finished speaking to Rainey and found out Safari had walked out on Gunzz. He plopped down into the plush leather sofa and kicked his feet up on the coffee table sighing. But then he thought to himself, maybe it wasn't a bad thing. She left out with Zeus, so he might be setting the job up for a go, real soon. After all, the contract on her is still good.

He glanced over at his cell phone, he still needed to pick Rainey's brain a little bit more. He needed to know where Safari kept her papers to the Corporation. Then they'd trick her into signing over the power to utilize Rainey in case of emergencies. In other words, the power of attorney. It wouldn't be any problems from that point once Rainey was in control of making her stupid ass sign over property, money…*thousands of dollars*, and eventually her seat on the board. But that was only if something were to happen to Safari. If he knew Zeus right, that wouldn't be too much longer.

He leaned back with his arms folded behind his head. A smile curled on his lips. He started thinking about Safari, then Rainey and how his manipulation game was still intact. He literally had Rainey wrapped around his finger. Safari would meet a sudden, ill-fated, quote-unquote accident. Getting killed by a jealous lover, Zeus. Then, he'd come in and kill Zeus and become a hero. Of course, he'd marry Rainey and she herself would meet an unexpected death, but only after the life insurance policy was put on her.

"Damn, what a fucking plan!" He grinned, then exhaled deeply and blew out slowly, relaxing.

"Chinese food tonight…or steak?" He asked himself out loud.

****

He was just about to tear into the exotic Bird soup he'd ordered when he heard the buzzing of his cell phone. He ignored it, figuring he'd answer it later on VM, but it continued on. He reached for it, it was Gunzz.

"Now what?" He sighed. "What's up, Boss?" He finally answered.

"*What's up, Boss*, my ass!"

Marcus shook his head. Gunzz was in his feelings and now he'd have to hear all the bullshit that went along with it. Shit, he had conjured up in his paranoid, delusional ass mind. After hearing him rant for the better part of fifteen minutes. Marcus figured he'd throw in the point to this whole thing.

"So, do we make the move on her now, or what?"

"That bitch! Who the hell does she think she is? I was about to give her ass a chance…but fuck it!"

"Okay, I'll get with Zeus…"

"Zeus…that bastard!"

"What are you talking about now?"

"I think he's trying to double-cross me! Get the girl for himself, then try to out me. What you think?"

Gunzz was evidently crazy, but Marcus couldn't believe how easy this was going to be. This had to be his day. Kill the girl, then Zeus. Wow! Maybe, even knock off Gunzz's stupid ass off in the throw.

"You know…you just might be right."

"Watch him, too!"

"Trust me…I will."

"Get back at me before you proceed, okay."

"Right. Now, uh, might take a few days, or so…"

"I understand, just do it!"

"Now, of course, the financial…"

"I got you, trust me."

"I would, but…business."

He could hear Gunzz blow into the phone. "One mill."

"*One mill?*"

"What, that's not enough?"

Marcus leaned back and glanced over at his TV, then said, "Look, I'm cleaning up after Zeus. Then, I'm taking out the trash on this whole thing. Literally, saving…your ass."

"Hmph, okay…okay. Then what?"

"Three mill…half now, the rest when the job is finished."

"Okay…okay!" Gunzz agreed. "Just do it."

After hanging up, Marcus picked up the remote control and surfed through some channels. He tuned in to mostly sports so he could catch up on the scores. He tossed his phone to the side and leaned into his meal. The phone buzzed again, but when he reached over this time, he turned it off. It was enough phone tag for the day.

****

Zeus got out and knocked on the door, like the gentleman he was trained by his Uncle to be. He wanted to let her know that he was sorry for how she felt earlier. He also wanted to make sure she'd gotten home safely.

55

He knocked, and after a while, she opened the door. "Why are you here?" she asked with her hands on her hips.

"Look, I'm sorry. It was nice meeting you, and I hope we have the opportunity again."

"I'm sure…we will."

Zeus turned and was about to walk back to his car when he heard her call his name. "Uh…yes?"

"Would you like to come in?"

"Well, I don't know if that's appropriate, Ms. Kennedy."

"Safari…please!" She turned and walked into the apartment leaving the door open.

Zeus exhaled, he really didn't want to at this time. But he'd at least get a chance to go in and check the place out. He'd have to anyway, but it would be a whole lot better if she wasn't in.

"When opportunity knocks," he joked.

Safari pointed him over to a sofa. "Please, have a seat." Zeus hesitantly did, and Safari got closer up on him. "Look, I just want a little company for a while. No, big thing, my nerves are still rattled from…*your boss*."

Zeus smiled. "I understand."

"Please, fix yourself a drink." She pointed towards the bar she had set up. "I'll be right back. Got to put on something a little more comfortable."

"Well, I can leave, and maybe come back."

"No silly!" Safari giggled. "I'm not putting on lingerie, or anything like that." She walked up the circular stairway to the upstairs half of the apartment that she shared with Rainey.

Once inside her bedroom, she leaned back against the door and let out a sigh.

"Okay, Safari," she whispered to herself. "Calm down and get yourself together." She sat down on her bed. "Damn, girl, he's fine as hell…but he's the enemy. He works for Gunzz, and I need to find out what Gunzz is trying to pull. Okay…okay!" She looked at her closet checking out outfits, then frowned. "No, too sexy, don't want to send the wrong message. Or look like I'm thirsty, or weak." Then she glanced over at her t-shirt, and sweatpants from earlier. "That's it, casual…but sexy."

She took off her heels and clothes then walked into the bathroom. Looking into the mirror she smiled, then took her hair out of the bun and let it drop. The silky long strands dropped past her shoulders and she started brushing them into curls.

"Yeah, girl, you can do this!"

Zeus sat comfortably on the sofa casually drinking on his Club soda. He didn't drink alcohol, he'd seen enough drunks coming up in his lifetime to detest it. He looked at it as a drug, a crutch. A crutch that eventually took the life of his Uncle Vervin. A crutch that cost his now deceased Uncle many of jobs. The apartment was pretty expensive for two single women. Somebody had some money coming in from somewhere. It had to be Safari. The other girl Rainey wasn't built like that. He remembered because he'd already cased their life and lifestyles. He knew Safari was the smartest of the two. He'd followed her a few times coming and going from her office on the College campus where she worked. He got up and walked over to the mantle above the fireplace where some pictures were set up.

"Must be her mother?" he silently questioned.

She was older yet very attractive, too. He looked closely at the others and almost spilled his drink. The man, there were pictures with the woman hugging him closely. Then, there were pictures of them and a little girl. It had to be her…Safari! Damn the guy he killed when he was young was this man. The girl, damn, that was the girl he'd let get away that day. He shook his head, then remembered what his Uncle said. The girl was the mark. Gunzz wanted her killed. Safari…was that girl. He backed up when he heard her door open from upstairs.

She walked down the stairway wearing the sweatpants, hugging her tight, shapely hips. She was built like a healthy ass athlete. He gasped at her beauty. She wore a collegiate t-shirt that was loose outside her pants and when he looked closely, she wore no bra. Her plump titties moved graciously from side to side as she moved, damn near hypnotizing him. Her hair swayed as the curls draped past her shoulders. She wore no makeup. She didn't need any as far as Zeus was concerned. She was the finest woman he'd ever seen. He looked in her eyes, then he noticed, yeah, she was that girl.

"Damn, what the hell did I get myself into?" he asked himself. He had to go see Gunzz, immediately.

"Everything alright?" she asked as she walked over to the bar. "You didn't get a drink?"

"Uh, no, I don't drink alcohol." He held up his glass. "Club soda is good."

"Okay, I don't either…drink hard liquor, that is. I do like my wine occasionally." She poured herself a glass of Chardonnay and walked over to where he was. "Okay, I see you're checking out the pictures." She pointed to her mother. "That's my mother."

"She's beautiful."

"Yes, she was."

"Was?"

"Yeah." Her mood became melancholic as she picked up the picture frame. "She was killed…car wreck."

"I'm sorry to hear that."

"Well…thank you."

Zeus pointed to the man in the photos. "And…him?"

"My father." She picked that frame up as well. "He was killed also…"

"Same car accident?"

"No… murdered."

"I'm so sorry."

"That's alright." She put it down, then walked to the sofa and sat, patting the seat next to her. "Have a seat."

Zeus turned her way. "Maybe, I'd better go, it's getting late." He glanced at his watch. "I'm sure you have something to do tomorrow."

"You're running away, that's so cute of you."

Zeus smiled. "No, I just don't want to impose..."

"You're not, trust me. I just want to talk for a minute. Cool?"

Zeus finally walked over and sat down, then faced her. "My boss…Gunzz, business?"

She swirled her wine around then said, "To be honest, I don't really know. I mean, you may know more than me."

"Actually...I don't."

"Well, I did my research…on your boss. I must say his past is very much undesirable."

"He's changed! I mean, he's a respected businessman now. He's even thinking about political office now. The people of St. Louis are behind him."

"Did he change? Or, did he manipulate the right people, then polish the right hands to get where he's at." She crossed her legs and Zeus couldn't help but admire her shape. The pants fit her snug and he couldn't see a ripple anywhere. Still, her intelligence mixed with this sexy demeanor. He'd never seen anything like this in a woman. "And, I'm sure he polished up on his smile."

"Perhaps." Zeus grinned.

They shared laughs, and small talk, then she looked in his face. His smile, his eyes, his handsome features, then she noticed.

"Hmmm, how'd you get that scar on your cheek?"

He rubbed at it, remembering that fateful day. He had to come up with a lie. "Uh, playing football when I was young."

"Damn, what did y'all play with…knives?"

They laughed again. They drank their drinks in silence at times. Stealing subtle glances at each other. Zeus broke the silence.

"I'd better go." He got up and she followed him to the door.

"I enjoyed your company," she said.

"Same here…Safari."

"I hope we can see each other again…maybe."

"Maybe."

She opened the door for Zeus, and he started to walk through. She grabbed his arm and pulled him towards her. Zeus hesitated at first, but her eyes, her smooth, chocolate skin, and her lips. Took all the fight out of him and they kissed. Her tongue darted in his mouth, his met hers and they wrestled with each other softly. He drew her closer and his dick got hard as all hell, she felt it and grinded up on him. Then, his mind took him where he didn't want to go. He had to kill her. That's was the contract. That was the job, and he pushed her gently away from him.

"I'm…I'm sorry!" He half smiled at her, then turned. "Goodnight Safari."

She watched as he walked to his car. He had swooped her up off her feet with that one kiss. She shut the door and leaned back against it thinking to herself.

'Be careful, Safari. You need to use him, and not fall for him. It's business!'

She walked up the stairs after cutting off the lights downstairs. When she got to her room she went into her walk-in closet. She pushed aside a vanity table revealing a safe behind it. She pressed in some numbers and it opened. On the bottom shelf were stacks of money. A couple of gees at best, and behind it was some paperwork, probably in connection to her Import/Export Corporation. She pulled out a briefcase from up top, put it on her bed and opened it. She retrieved a nasty .40 Caliber automatic. She ran her hands across the fine lines of steel and glanced at the gas charged silencer next to it and thought about Gunzz, then Zeus.

"Yeah, it was business…just business," she told herself.

Zeus cruised along Highway 40 thinking about Safari. That this was the girl he'd let get away. But he couldn't help it, he liked her then, and even more now. Her conversation, her demeanor. He was definitely falling for her, but he couldn't. She was the mark! He shook his head, he had to get it together. He'd get up with Gunzz tomorrow and find out more about the job. Her and her father because that one kiss damn sure changed the game. *Big time!*

LOVIN' SAFARI

CHAPTER 8

Rainey had slipped into the apartment during the early morning hour after a night out club hopping. Her eyes were bloodshot red, most likely from the drinks, and a little weed. Her pants were soiled around the crotch, more than likely from a sexual encounter, or two knowing her. She fumbled around the keyhole with her keys, and upon entering pressed her personal pin numbers into the security box. She leaned back and belched. She walked around quietly so she would not wake Safari. She really didn't want to hear none of her self-righteous bullshit this morning. She glanced over at the bar and eyeballed the Scotch.

"Just one more drink would do it," she said to herself.

Then, she'd take a shower maybe, and crash. As far as she knew, she, nor Safari didn't have anything to do or anywhere to go today.

"Yep, that's the plan," she giggled. "Sleep in late."

She tiptoed into the room past the sofa and that's when she heard slight snoring, Safari's. She was cuddled up in a blanket on the couch. She looked around at the TV, it wasn't on, but she was probably watching it before she dozed off. The remote was on the floor in front of her. She was out like a light. Rainey waved off the liquor and turned around going upstairs. She really didn't want to disturb her. Looking upstairs, she noticed that Safari's room door was slightly opened and the light on.

After trudging up the steps in forced silence, she peeked in and saw that all was well, then when she turned around to turn out the light, she saw it. Still on the bed was the briefcase with Safari's gun. Rainey peeped downstairs and she was still sleeping, hard. She dipped into the room and stared at the gun. She didn't know what it was, but she knew it was real.

"Is this Safari's?" she asked quietly. "Naw, it can't be. She's way too much of a goody-goody to even deal with this type of weaponry." Rainey shook her head in confusion, then shrugged it off.

She turned toward the bathroom and noticed her closet was wide open too. Now she was just going to be just plain ole nosey. Maybe, steal an outfit or two. Hell, she'd never miss it. She stepped in and that's when she noticed the vanity table was moved aside and the safe behind it was open. She crept over and looked in. Money, lots of it, but that wasn't unusual for Safari. She had it like that. The top shelf was empty, but she noticed some folders in the back behind the stacks of cash. She reached in and pulled one out.

A brown leather folder with gold embroidery entitled Wildlife Import/Export Corporation…Safari's corporation. She opened it and thumbed through the papers, bonds, and securities. She closed that one put it back and pulled out the other. Opening it, she saw the legal documents that were proof of ownership, all other Legalities, and Offshore accounts. Stuff that she damn sure wouldn't want to get into the wrong hands, but hell, Rainey wasn't the wrong hands. She was her best friend.

Rainey smiled, she'd hit the jackpot. These were the papers that Marcus wanted. Cuffing them she turned and started back out of the room, then heard Safari grumble and move around downstairs, and she froze. Safari had just turned over and went back to sleep. Rainey walked softly towards her room and slipped in. She locked her door and pulled out her cell phone. Granted, it was early, but she had to let him know. She hit contacts looking up the name: Marcus.

****

Zeus got up and went through his usual routine. A morning workout, that consisted of a three-mile run. He had a lot on his mind. When he got back in, he showered, then started up a fresh pot of coffee. After sitting down enjoying a quick breakfast, he glanced at his cell phone. He needed to call Gunzz and make an appointment to see him today. He had to ask him about the job and Safari.

Gunzz was a paranoid man and he knew he'd have to go to his Mansion strapped. He sighed, now he needed to call Marcus to be his backup. He really didn't want to include him in on this yet, but he had no choice. Someone had to have his back. He reached over for another cup of coffee then reached for the cell phone.

"Here we go with the bullshit," he grumbled as he speed dialed the number.

LOVIN' SAFARI

CHAPTER 9

Zeus jumped in the ride and drove over to Marcus' place. On the way, he drove through their old stomping grounds, the block, and his old school. He reminisced on the times he and Marcus ran from the thugs and bullies that terrorized the impoverished, ghetto neighborhood. He was sure glad his uncle started working them into the business at such a young age. In high school, they'd become focused, maybe not on school, but their minds where sharp and Vervin took full advantage. It, however, didn't help with their studies, but they weren't dumb either.

They were able to hone their fighting skills and put down a couple of key bullies in the process. Their charismatic skills worked a whole lot better for them though. They had girls and popularity. Soon enough the whole bully thing was past them. Marcus excelled in sports, basketball, football, and track. He was also the ladies man of the two.

Zeus was quiet and reserved he was athletic as well, but he preferred to be behind the scenes as opposed to being out there. Once his mother passed away, and then his uncle, he felt alone. Other than Marcus, his friends were few, and far in between. His lust for the hot ass, young girls that ran around in his circles didn't faze him.

He didn't want to take his old man's path. Then leave a mother with children and no means of support. His uncle eventually rectified the problem with that, but Zeus still lacked that something in his heart. His other siblings Randy, and Geraldine eventually moved away once they were old enough. Randy went to school and became a physical therapist, then he moved to New York. His sister Geraldine married a guy from California. He became an LAPD, and she moved out there with him.

They remained in touch, Zeus was still the big brother, and he showed his love for family by showering his nieces and nephews with gifts. His siblings never asked what he actually did to acquire his finances, but they somewhat had an idea that it wasn't legal. Zeus for the most to them was good. They'd call in and check on him from time to time, and he'd do the same.

The last time he'd seen them was at his Uncle Vervin's funeral. He promised them then he'd leave St. Louis and settle down. That's where his mind was at now as he passed by the cemetery where they were buried. He was tired of Gunzz, and the low-level jobs he was getting. They paid good but lacked the caliber for his skills and this was the worse thus far. He was falling off, he'd started to like this woman…the mark.

He still couldn't believe it was the same girl from when he was a kid. But St. Louis wasn't that damn big anyway, so what was he to expect? He knew he'd see her one day, but just not like this. He rubbed his hand unconsciously across his scar.

Zeus pulled up in front of Marcus' apartment and blew the horn. Then Marcus' came bopping out. He had to smile, Marcus always had that pretty boy type of swag. Once Unc trained him, and he got all his get back from the thugs who'd bullied him, he never looked back. He wore flex distressed denim jeans, and a form-fitting, cardigan cowl sweater. He was tight. Far from the young kid that would run from the bullies in his hood. Marcus reached for the door, then looked up and cheesed at the ladies who suddenly appeared out of nowhere in lingerie on the terraces of the expensive condo he shared with them.

"Horny asses!" Zeus shook his head and laughed.

Marcus straightened up and gave them the view they wanted, him. "What's up?" he said getting in the car. "Looking good…fresh! Worked out, huh?"

"Little something."

"You always say that." Marcus laughed. "You've got the fuckin' build of a linebacker, and just as quick. Yet, you always shrug it off like it's nothing." He pointed to the ladies in the balconies. "You see that they want cats like us." He waved at them.

Zeus grinned. "But do I want women like them?" He looked around at them. "Too thirsty for me."

"Well, I can stand to quench their thirst every now and then."

Laughing their way up the boulevard, they leaned back, and Marcus said, "Damn, this Cadillac rides smooth as hell."

"CTS…yeah…it does."

Marcus turned down the music they were listening to and turned towards him. "Look, uh, you know Gunzz is concerned about the job."

"Like what?"

"Well, I mean…the girl."

Zeus sighed. "That's what this meeting is about."

"So, what's the deal?"

Zeus looked around for a place to pull the car over so they could talk. When he did, he pushed the seat back some, then said, "The girl, there's something about her."

"Something?"

"I mean, she has class and style. We can talk and she just relaxes me so damn much."

"Damn, you like her?"

"Yeah…I guess I do."

Marcus sighed. "Look, that's all good. But the bad part of this is she's the mark. You're being paid to kill her."

"I understand that trust me, I do. But maybe I can change that."

"What…not kill her?"

"Buy her contract. Find out why he wants her killed, then maybe change the situation. I mean, knowing Gunzz it's probably all a money thing."

Marcus shook his head. "But suppose it's not, suppose it's personal?"

"Well, I got to at least find out."

Marcus turned and leaned back, then spazzed. "Man, Zeus, you're fucking up! This is a job, we're in the business. Muthafucka's like us don't live those happily ever after type stories. We fuck them up!"

"Maybe, this time it could be different?"

"Different how? He paid you to do a job! You got to either do it, or someone else will."

Zeus paused and took a deep breath, that hit him hard. What he was saying was true, but he had to at least try. "I can at least try…"

"Fuck that! You sound like a pussy, all in your feelings. You got a job to do. You think a smart ass, educated, bougie ass woman gonna go for you? Yeah, you got money, but these women got class. They cut from a different mold. We from the muthafuckin' bottom. She went to school to get her bread. You just killed a bunch of muthafuckas!"

Zeus turned and frowned. "So, what?"

"*So, what?*" Marcus waved his hand at him in jest. "You don't get it, do you? You honestly think she can go for you?"

"Why not me?"

"C'mon man, get real. She's got a Corporation…a degree…"

"So, you saying she's smarter than me?"

Marcus looked at his friend and sighed. "Yeah, bruh, that's exactly what I'm saying."

"You think you're better than me too, huh?"

Marcus shook his head. "Man…I went to school. I mingled with the right people. All you did was train…and kill people."

"Motherfucka, I made it possible for you to be who you are. I made you!"

"Yeah…true, you did. You the man I always wanted to be, so, I got what you got. The training, but I always rubbed elbows with…the right people. Hell, I put you on to more than a few jobs. And now, you want to throw all that shit away…for some pussy. That's crazy!"

Zeus pulled the seat up and cranked up the car, then pulled on into the boulevard. "Yeah…crazy…"

"Look, Zeus, I didn't mean to…"

"Me and my Uncle gave you a set of balls. And, you think they're bigger than mine." He turned his way when they got to a red light. "We gonna see…trust me."

Marcus didn't respond, it was done. They both knew how each other felt. After this job, they would go their own separate ways. At this rate that would be real soon.

LOVIN' SAFARI

CHAPTER 10

Gunzz stood by the window looking out in thought, his mind all over the place. He stared across at the St. Louis Monument. Across from it was his old stomping grounds, where it all began. Now, here he was years later overlooking St. Louis in a shiny, steel and glass skyscraper. He'd managed to grease enough palms, extort, and blackmail people into investing in his own Bonding Company.

It made money, not as lucrative, but it was a nice front. It was the drugs and prostitution he funneled into the city from Chicago that made him well off. The business just washed money. Now, he had lots of finances and needed to make more grown-up investments.

That's where Safari would come into play. If he could convince her to let him in on the Board of Directors of her Wildlife Import/Export Corporation, he could perhaps go legit. Better yet, if he were to somehow get her interested in him romantically then they could be partners. He wouldn't mind either if his role was silent, as long as the bread was right. He'd make sure she had all the comforts a woman could need. Then she'd refine him and make him a legit man instead of a two-bit gangster.

He stared outward thinking it all sounded so good, but now there was a hitch in the plans…Zeus. Granted, he wanted to kill the woman at first, but he also wanted the pussy…bad. Then if that didn't pan out, perhaps then he'd kill her, then coerce his way onto the Board himself. He had an inside man. The same inside man that told him he could put him in Safari's seat if she just happened to disappear.

That was the plan as far as Zeus was concerned. The contract to kill her, and eliminate the body was hefty. Zeus wanted two-million, the price of a quiet job, and that's what Gunzz was willing to pay.

Now, all of a sudden Zeus was into the woman. Was it a double cross, Gunzz wondered? He had to stop the bullshit quickly if that was the case. Marcus was his next option.

"Hell, let Marcus kill them," he said.

He could always find himself another chick. His distorted scheming mind made it all sound so rational, but it was the thoughts of a sick man: a two-bit gangster.

The intercom buzzed on the desk and he turned around and pressed it. "Yes!"

"You have, Mr. Zeus and Mr. Marcus here to see you."

"Okay, let them in."

"Yes, sir."

He pulled out the chair to his desk and waited. He had a half-ass idea what Zeus wanted to talk about. Nine times out of ten, and he'd bet good money it was going to be about Safari. Questions about why, he never put him all the way into the loop, but Gunzz really didn't think he needed to be.

Zeus and Marcus walked through the door.

"Gentlemen, what brings the both of you here, uptown?" Gunzz asked.

Zeus walked over to the desk and shook his hand. "I wanted to discuss…uh, talk about something."

Marcus stood behind him, he acknowledged Gunzz by a wave of the hand then sat on the sofa off to the side of the decorative office.

"Okay. You want a drink?"

"No, I'm alright," Zeus answered.

"Marcus?"

Marcus nodded, and Gunzz pointed him to the bar. "I know you'd like a Scotch."

"Yep," Marcus said as he reached into the bar and pulled out a glass. "Hope we didn't interrupt anything."

"Naw."

Marcus sat back down while Zeus pulled up a chair in front of the desk.

"You don't mind, do you?" Zeus asked looking at Gunzz.

"No! Now, what's up gentlemen?"

Zeus sat back and crossed his legs. He paused before speaking. He wanted to make sure Gunzz would get a full understanding of what he was about to say. It was bad enough he was questioning him about the job, much less on a personal issue.

"This job."

"The woman."

"Yeah…Ms. Kennedy."

"Oh, Safari, that's her name, right?"

Zeus cleared his throat and cut an eye at Marcus. "Yeah…uh, I understand the contract. In a nutshell, take her out and dispose of the body cleanly."

"Yes, that's the contract…what I'm paying for."

"From what I know of her, so far, maybe that might not be necessary."

"Not necessary!" Gunzz snarled. "Why is that?"

"Maybe, she can be utilized. After all, she runs a pretty lucrative business."

"Okay."

"I was thinking maybe we could let this one go."

"Let it go?" Gunzz leaned forward on the desk. "But I paid you."

"You did, I can give you that back."

"Give me back…one mill?" He sighed, then swiveled his chair around towards the window. "But all this cost me time *and* money." He reached into his suit vest pocket and pulled out a stout cigar. "It's worth way more than that Zeus. Come on now, you been around me long enough. You know when I order a hit, there's something more on the line than money."

"I know, I thought maybe I could throw in a little extra, for your inconvenience, of course."

"Of course," Gunzz said as he lit the cigar and blew the smoke into the air. "But you see…" He turned back around facing him. "…I needed this to be done. You know Zeus, I really don't understand. Marcus, do you understand this?"

"Well…" Marcus took a sip of the drink and looked over at Zeus. "…from what I understand. He feels some sort of way for the girl…"

"I do," Zeus butted in. "Let's not beat around the bush. Let's get straight to it."

"Then, get straight to it."

"I, uh…I have been seeing Ms. Kennedy, and we have an understanding."

"An understanding?" He snickered. "What the fuck is that?" He looked over at Marcus and gave him a side look. "Hell, I just thought you were fucking her."

"It's more than that."

"Is it?" Gunzz stood up. "You see, I'm thinking maybe you were just fucking her. Then, as a result, she confided in you. Maybe, told you somethings…about the business and me. That's what I'm thinking, Zeus. Explain this shit to me better."

"Well Gunzz, I want to buy her contract. Terminate it and possibly set things right with her. I'll do whatever you want…"

"You muthafuckin' right you'll do whatever." He leaned on the desk. "Listen, you're a fucking assassin, Zeus. You kill people. What the fuck would you do with a chick like that?"

"I told his ass that," Marcus laughed.

"Well, he should have listened. Either do it, or someone else will!" Gunzz sat back down. "I'm giving you a fucking week. We made a deal, Zeus…*a deal*!" He turned Marcus' way. "Don't go back on your word, you hear!"

Zeus had a feeling it would turn out this way. "Gunzz, I did a lot for you, put in a lot of work. I'm asking you this one time, let this one go. I'll take care of it for you. I'll make sure she does what's needed to get you on the Board."

"You!" Gunzz laughed. "Oh, you will. Fuck all the hired people I have in place. What are going to do, fuck her into compliance?" He laughed harder and looked over at Marcus again. "What the fuck is this nigga thinking, Marcus?"

Zeus stood up, he was pissed. Not just at the way, Gunzz was clowning him, but because it didn't work out the way he'd wanted. He couldn't kill Safari, and right now, Gunzz knew it. This was definitely going to be a problem. He had a week max to figure this out, somehow.

"I hear you," he said, then looked over at Marcus. "You coming?"

Marcus got up and shrugged his shoulders, then walked over to the bar and poured another drink. Then he walked over to the desk where Gunzz was sitting at. "Naw…I'm staying."

Zeus just nodded his head. It was then he realized that Marcus would be the one Gunzz would pay to do the job if he didn't. Another thing he knew for sure was that he'd fucked up by telling Marcus how he felt about Safari. So now, if Marcus was going to get the job done, he'd have to kill him, too.

Zeus just walked to the door with his head hung down and said, "I'll let myself out."

"You do that," Gunzz said. "And…if you're not going to do the job, I need one-point-five."

"*One-point-five?*"

"Mill, that's the cost for fucking me over. Nothing personal Zeus, just business."

Zeus glanced his way before he closed the door and said, "Yeah…business!"

CHAPTER 11

Zeus stood in front of the solid wood door for a minute, wrapping his head around the speech he was about to give Safari. He wanted to confess his love, and at the same time let her in on his reason for even knowing her, and how they got to this point. It was funny, he'd killed many men in cold blood and thought nothing of it, literally had nerves of steel. Now, here it was they were raveled. He was trying to muster up the nerve to let this woman know that he cared for her. His feelings were about to be exposed, and he felt vulnerable.

He wanted to do this, however, uncomfortable he was. He was tired of being lonely. Tired of looking over his shoulder all the time. Tired of one-night stands with women he didn't know, or for that matter didn't even know him. But Marcus had also put negative thoughts in his head. Maybe, he was right, maybe, he wasn't meant to be with a woman like her.

Even though he was cultivated so far as into what he learned to be able to stalk his victims. To be able to maneuver in the prestigious environments she frequented. But for him to have to evolve into that status it would be a lot overwhelming for him. However, for her, he reasoned it was worth a shot.

He rang the doorbell and could hear her coming to the door. From the tapping of heels to tile he could tell she wore stilettos and was probably all dressed up. He'd called her earlier and told her he was coming by. She probably thought maybe they would go out to eat or something. He didn't mind that, but he wanted to let her know what was going on first.

"Hello," she chimed after opening the door. She turned to pick up her purse and Zeus stopped her. "What's wrong?" she asked.

"Nothing, nothing at all." He came through the door and kissed her. "I just wanted to talk, for a few."

Safari could tell from his earnestness that he was serious. "Oh, okay. Is everything alright?"

Zeus held her hand, guided her to the sofa, and she sat. "You want a drink?" he asked.

"No…I'm okay. What's going on, Zeus?"

He grabbed a glass and poured a club soda, then sat down next to her. "There's something I need to tell you."

She crossed her legs and turned his way. "Yes!"

"Now, there's no need to be alarmed."

"Zeus…what is it?"

He reached into his jacket and pulled out a small, black velvet cube, causing her eyes to widen. "This is for you." He opened it and the glimmer from the white diamond ring sparkled in her eyes.

She gasped. "Zeus…it's too much!"

"No…not enough," he corrected.

She reached out and picked it up out of the case.

"Zeus…this is too much!"

He got up, then took a knee. "Safari…I want to marry you."

Safari grabbed at her heart, then clasped her hands. "You hardly know me!"

"I know enough about you to know that I'm making the right decision."

"Oh, Zeus…"

"The moments we've shared…the love…the bond between us…intimate bond!"

"She rubbed her hand around his face tenderly. "I want that…but…"

Zeus sighed. "*But?*"

"What about you? I mean, you know things about me, and I really don't know that much about you."

He nodded. "True, and, that's what I wanted to talk about." He slid the ring on her finger. "This is yours…regardless."

Safari leaned into him as Zeus got back up. He kissed her lips, and sat back, then took a drink from his club soda. "What you do know is that I work for, Gunzz Black."

"Yes."

"What you really don't know is what I do."

"Well…yeah, that's true. I thought maybe you were an associate of his… a partner?"

"No, I'm contracted by, Gunzz Black."

"Contracted?"

"I'm contracted to eliminate threats on behalf of, Gunzz Black."

"*Threats*, I don't understand."

"I'm a hit man…a hired assassin." Safari's mouth dropped and she eased back from him. Zeus could see the fear in her eyes. "I used to be…" He reached for her hand and she pulled it back.

"*Used to be*!" She eased back further. "So…that's what you were going to do to me?"

"Not anymore…"

"How do I know that?"

"I'm telling you…the truth."

She picked up a pillow and eased it in front of her. Zeus could see her eyes as they darted around the room looking for something to defend herself with. "Please…stay back."

"Safari…it's okay."

"*Okay*! You tell me you love me, but you wanted to kill me. How is that okay?"

"Because I called the whole thing off. I confronted, Gunzz and told him it wasn't going to happen…"

"*Not by you*, but suppose he gets someone else. *Oh, my god*! He wants to kill me." Safari started breathing heavy, trying to control the panic attack she was about to have.

Zeus pushed up on her. "Calm down, Safari, you've got to believe me…*trust me!*"

"Trust you?" She bounced up out of her seat. "You were going to kill me, and you want me to trust you?"

"Safari, please, listen! It's not like that anymore."

"Why!"

"Because…I bought your contract!" Zeus got up, walked toward her front window and peered out the curtains. "I'm giving him back the money, and then some for him to leave it, and you alone."

Safari sighed. "Can you trust him?" She eased closer, and very cautiously toward him.

"I really don't know."

"Well, suppose he reneges on his word?"

Zeus turned and faced her. "That's what I think, too. That's why I wanted to give him money, and then…"

"*Then what?*"

"Then, go away for a while…kinda disappear until it blows over."

She reached for him, hugged him, then kissed him tenderly on the lips. "Are you sure?"

He looked into her eyes. "I'm not going to let anything happen to you, I promise."

Safari kissed him. "Okay…let me handle some affairs quick, then I'll pack."

"Okay, I'll be right here, but be quick." She turned and rushed up the stairs, and then hollered downstairs at him. *"My bags are in the garage! Can you grab them?"*

Zeus turned to go into the garage, and Safari watched. When he was out of sight, she dipped into her closet, pushed back the vanity desk, and opened her safe. She reached in and grabbed the money, then reached towards the back for her folders. She grabbed one, then when she reached for the other, she noticed it was missing.

"What the hell!" She grabbed her gun case and put it on the bed. She sat wondering where the other files were. Her Ownership, and Governance papers for her corporation. Then, she figured it all out. The night when she passed out on the couch, she must have left the safe open. Rainey came in late that night she remembered and probably saw the safe open.

"Damn!" She frowned. "Rainey has the goddamned folder. What the hell was she up to?"

Zeus had come back in. "Here they are, I'll bring them up."

"Hold up. Can you look in my closet downstairs and grab a few, uh…jackets?"

"Jackets? We can buy more jackets!"

"Pleeeassse Zeus!"

"Okay…okay." He shook his head. "Women!" he mumbled under his breath.

Safari then grabbed a bag from under her bed and stuffed the money and papers inside of it. She opened up her briefcase, took the gun out, loaded it and pushed it under her pillow. Zeus was on his way up the stairs. She dipped back in the closet with the briefcase and shoved it back into the safe. She closed it and moved the table back in time just as Zeus made it through her bedroom door.

"Here you go."

She peeped her head out of the closet. "Thank you, Sweetie."

Zeus got closer to her and pushed up on her. "We got a little time…" he said.

She pulled him closer when she looked over his shoulder at the butt of the gun that showed underneath her pillow. She grabbed him and led him towards the bathroom with his back away from it.

"Not yet baby…I've got things to do. Later!" she said.

Zeus kissed her. "Okay, later!" He turned and walked out of the room.

Safari rushed over to the bed, covered up the gun better, and sighed. "What do I do?" she asked herself quietly. "Think girl…think!"

She knew one thing for sure, she was going to keep the gun with her because, right now, too much was taking place, and she wasn't about to be a statistic. Not anymore!

****

Marcus pulled up in front of the condo. He was stopping by to see Rainey. She kept calling, and texting saying she'd found what he was looking for.

"About time," he said to himself. He honked the horn expecting her to come out, but she didn't. He picked up his phone and dialed her number.

Zeus peeked outside the curtains just as Safari called downstairs to him.

"That must be, Rainey's friend," Safari said.

Zeus couldn't believe it. "You know him?"

"Met him a few times. He's been messing around with, Rainey."

"Shit!" Zeus spat.

"What?" Safari eased down the steps. "What is it now?"

Zeus crept away from the curtains. "That's, Gunzz's goon…Marcus."

"You serious?"

"Very," Zeus replied.

He reached into his jacket, and his holster was empty. He shot a glance at the window and realized he'd left his gun in the car. He got closer and peeked out again. Marcus was on the phone when he saw the curtains ease back, he honked the horn again.

Zeus looked up the street, his car was parked in front of another condo. That was the only spot available at the time. He sighed, that was the one thing that would stop Marcus from coming in, and suspecting he was there.

Safari brushed up behind Zeus and he flinched. "What's going on, Zeus?" she asked. "You're scaring me!"

He had to think fast. "I need you to go to the door, and see what he wants," Zeus instructed.

"Why?"

"Baby…" He pulled her closer. "…just do it, trust me."

"Okay." She took a deep breath, walked to the door. and opened it. "Yes!" She called out.

Marcus couldn't get ahold of Rainey, and he was frustrated. He peeked his head out the window and put on his pretty boy smile. "Hey, how are you, is Rainey there?"

"Uh..." Safari peeked over to the window. Marcus followed her eyes and saw the curtain move. Someone was in there with her. "...no, she stepped out earlier." He started to get out, but she said, "I'm about to take a shower, then call it a night." She faked a yawn.

"Oh, okay. When she comes back in, have her call me, please."

"I will." Safari closed the door.

He knew something was up because it didn't feel right. His phone buzzed suddenly, and he reached for it. It was Rainey. "Where are you?"

"I'm uptown, wanted to buy some wine. Where are you?"

"Why didn't you pick up the damn phone?"

"I was busy. Why?"

"You got those papers?"

"I told you I have them."

"On you?"

"No…they're at the house."

Marcus banged the steering wheel with his fist, and it honked loudly. He scanned the neighborhood making sure he didn't spook anyone. That's when he saw it, Zeus' car parked up the street.

"Hmmm…okay." He looked at the condo checking out the alleyway leading to the back going past the garage. He spoke back into the phone. "Look, go ahead, and do your thing. I'll call you back later, then come pick you up. Cool?"

"Uh, sure, okay. I'll just hang out here."

"Okay." He hung up abruptly.

Marcus was an asshole, but Rainey knew something was up, too. He was always rude, but this time she felt a vibe. She reached into her pocket and dialed Safari.

Safari's phone vibrated: both she and Zeus stared at it. "Don't pick it up, it might be him."

She got closer and looked at the screen. "It's just, Rainey." She reached for it.

Zeus stopped her. "No, he might be setting you up. Just be cool." She eased back toward the stairs, and Zeus said, "Go upstairs and finish getting your things together."

Zeus slid closer to the window and kept an eye on Marcus wondering why he hadn't pulled off yet. If he tried to break in, they'd have to fight.

Marcus reached into the glove compartment and pulled out his .9mm auto, then screwed the silencer that was with on. He cranked up the car and drove away opposite of Zeus' car. He didn't want to let on that he knew he was in there. He figured he'd come back later when it was dark, then make his move. Until then, he'd wait.

Zeus watched the car as he finally pulled off, then hollered up to Safari. "*Hurry up, I got a feeling he's trying to set you up!*" He knew because he'd taught him, and that's what he would have done.

Safari dipped quickly into her room and grabbed a few things, throwing them into a Gucci bag. Then got undressed and bounced into the shower. Zeus came up the stairs and stood next to the door, figuring to himself that he might as well wait until it got dark before they hauled ass.

CHAPTER 12

Night was soon approaching, and Zeus sat on the couch by Safari's bed waiting for her to come out of the shower. His mind was fixated on where they should run to. He was contemplating Brazil. The weather was good this time of the year, and he had enough cash to lamp for a good minute.

"Yeah," he nodded. "That sounds like a plan." He was still in his thoughts when Safari stepped out of the bathroom, causing him to gasp.

She wore a plush rose-colored, silk lingerie, that hugged at her body. The beads of water from the wetness of the shower didn't help matters as the coolness swelled up her nipples. Her hair tumbled like a waterfall cascading down her back reaching the crack of her ass. The slinky fabric of her top shined in the glimmer of the moonlight, and it fit like new skin to her luscious body.

She turned and looked his way. "What's wrong?"

Zeus blinked out of his trance. "Nothing…not a damn thing."

He got up and walked toward her. Her eyes were the eyes of innocence, they were full, chinkie and doe-like. The clear whites of her eyes made him melt as he reached out to her and she reached back. He kissed her and ran his hands down the sides of her waist, then he glided his hands smoothly along her swollen ass. She pulled at him when she did his dick hardened. He stepped back and commenced to taking off his clothes.

She sat down admiring his smooth, chocolate complexion, as he playfully threw the shirt at her. She giggled, then leaned back taking in his muscular body, which made her horny and wet. Once he had his pants off, he stood, letting her admire the hard, earned work he put into his body.

"Pull the muthafuckin' covers back." She obeyed, then leaned back onto the pillows. "Take those goddamned panties off!"

She slowly, and purposely slid out of the thongs she wore, and exposed her luscious, full pussy to him. He moved forward toward her. Safari was hot just from submitting to his demands.

"Hand me those panties!"

She eased them off, then slung them toward the edge of the bed. He quickly snatched up the wet thongs and sniffed them. "We're going to do this my way," he said smiling.

"Okay, baby…whatever you want…" Without warning, he grabbed her left wrist and put it behind her back, securing it with the lace from her panties, then secured the right.

Bound with both hands behind her back now, Safari leaned forward parting her lips in fiery arousal from the swollen erection of the man she was now craving.

"Oohhh, Zeus!" she purred.

Eye to eye with his dick, she went tongue first as her lips swallowed the head whole. Then, she spit it out, and delicately licked the tip. Taking it out once again, she spit on the head teasing him with a mean tongue swirl as if she were savoring the flavor. Zeus plunged the head deeper, and inch by inch she took him into her mouth until she gagged, then let out a moan.

She stopped long enough to look up at him and say, "Feed it to me…baby!" Then she opened her mouth wider and let her lips, and saliva work the shaft and base of his dick, along with his balls all at the same time.

Zeus was glassy eyed as his chest rose and fell the moment, he dug his hands into her head, ruffling her hair. He rocked feverishly back and forth. Willingly, Safari allowed him to literally fuck her face. He started rough and rugged like the gangster he was, then slowed down becoming gentle and passionate exposing his gentleman side. He slipped in and out of her throat, then went into overdrive.

"*Safari…oohhh, shit, Safari!*" He yelled out.

Head bobbing up and down, Safari sucked with pure energy, and excitement, enjoying every inch. His moaning and begging her to slow down had her dripping wet between her legs. Then, just as he reached his tipping point, he pulled out. Without a word, he turned her face down onto the bed, positioned her doggy style and smacked her ass.

"Come to muthafuckin' Daddy!" he commanded.

"*Ooohhh shit!*" she cried out, wriggling her cheeks. "Do it again!" He smacked it again. "Shiiiittt!"

Zeus kneeled, spread her cheeks, and peeled her lips apart. Then he started kissing her clit.

Safari hollered out. "Oh, my god…give it to me Zeus!"

Zeus grabbed her tied wrist, pulled her to him until the crack of her ass was at the head of his dick, and arched her back. Safari could do nothing but toot that thing up.

"Fuck me, Zeus!" she begged.

He entered her and sunk deep into her moist pussy. His action along with the force of his thrusts was already enough to bring her to an orgasm. Stroke after stroke, she matched his thrusts. The pussy was slippery and good, Zeus felt like he was fucking hot butter. Her passion and her roar were like a lioness in heat. He shifted his stance, reached down and pinched her clit hard.

That catapulted her all the way there.

"I'm…cummmiiinnn!" she squealed loudly.

He snatched at her wrist, pounded harder, and shuddered. Safari let out a gargled cry as she clamped her pussy around his dick and came hard.

Zeus pulled out and came all over her ass. "You're… definitely…keeping that ring," he stuttered exhaustedly.

****

"Danika, have my car pulled around the front," Gunzz spoke into the intercom.

"Alright. Stepping out, sir?" Danika commented.

"Yeah."

"Want me to hold any appointments for the day?"

"Yeah, gotta feeling it's gonna be a long one."

"Okay, sir. Uh, do you need me for the rest of the day?"

Gunzz looked down at the intercom and smiled. "No, Danika, go home and give the kids a hug."

"Yes, sir."

Danika had been around Gunzz for a minute. Once considered a hood rat, Gunzz took a nonsexual liking to her. He just had a good feeling about her and took her in. She was barely twenty-five with five children. She'd thought about giving them all up so they could at least have a better future than what she could give. It reminded Gunzz of his own mother, and siblings, and how hard it was for them.

When he opened up his Bonding business, he let her run the office. She didn't have the schooling, but hell Gunzz figured. Since she had five children, she was just as good as anyone else.

He'd made a good choice. She was hella loyal, and he paid

her well as a result. Her oldest had just started college and she was excited and antsy as all hell like any proud mom would be.

The intercom buzzed. "Excuse me, sir. Do you want me to call your, uh…friend?"

Gunzz turned and walked to the window looking out at his car drive around out front. "No, Danika, that's alright. I think she'll be expecting me."

"Okay, sir, have a good day."

"You too, Danika."

Gunzz started toward the door, then stopped and turned back around staring at his desk. He rubbed his chin and thought for a second, then doubled back. He opened a bottom drawer, reached in the back and pulled out his gun.

"Like American Express, don't leave home without it," he said to himself.

Once he was in the Maybach, his driver cranked up and asked where he was going. Gunzz told him to hold on for a minute. He pulled out his phone, dialed some numbers and waited for an answer.

The person he called picked up. "Hey…wassup?"

He listened attentively to what they were saying. "Oh…okay." He leaned back in his seat. "So, you want me to pick you up...or meet you there?" He leaned forward towards his driver waiting for his answer. "Okay then." Tossing the sleek iPhone to the side, he said to his driver. "Downtown…"

Rainey sat at the Overview Cafe over on Market Street and North 14th drinking another cocktail. She had a few bags from shopping at a cute little boutique she'd spied. Her feet were weary from the heels she wore. She thought maybe Marcus would have been there already. She'd called a few times and it went straight to voicemail. She was ready to go home.

The waitress came over again and asked if she wanted to order any food. She shook her head but could see from the reaction on her face, she was taking up a seat from a tip paying customer. It was time to go. She finished her drink, got up and walked toward the front door. She pulled out her cellphone and made a call.

"I'm on my way home. Okay…okay, I'll see you then," she said.

She doubled back, sat a few dollars down at her table for the waitress, smiled and then left. It would only take a few minutes to get home. She knew waving down a cab wouldn't be difficult. She had to come up with a plan though. She needed to be able to snatch up the files she stole from Safari, and dip back out quickly, and quietly. Hopefully, she wasn't there. She felt bad about cutting her throat, but she was hellbent on living the lifestyle she swore Safari had stolen from her.

Ever since her family took her in, it was as if Rainey herself became a step-child of sorts. Safari's money helped pay the bills, and her parents put her on a pedestal. Rainey didn't lack for anything, except attention. A few minutes later, the cab pulled up in front of the house, she paid the driver, scooped up her bags and got out. She peeped a little at the curtain as she headed up the walkway, it was ruffled some. That wasn't Safari's style, she was so adamant about neatness, it was like she had OCD or something. Suddenly, her phone started vibrating. She reached into her bag, pulled it out, and checked the screen.

It was Marcus. "Hey, Marcus, sweetheart. I couldn't wait so I…"

"Yeah, I see."

She turned and looked around. She didn't see him or his car. "Where are you at?" She looked at the window. "You inside?"

"No, not yet. You…uh, gonna get those files, right?"

"Yeah, of course, I told you that."

"Okay."

"You coming by to pick me back up. I'll only be a minute."

"I will, but first you got to get back out. Your roommate is there, Safari."

"Oh, okay." She stuck her key in the door, then opened it. "And, so is…"

Stepping through she looked up and Safari was standing on the stairs looking down at her. It startled her, and she cut Marcus off. "Gotta go…call you back." She came in and set her bags down. "Hey! Didn't know you were here. How are you?" she said staring at Safari.

Safari started walking towards the stairway. "I'm fine…you?"

Safari didn't want to let her in on the fact that she knew she'd been through her things. "Hey, have you seen my Louboutin's?"

"No." Rainey picked her bags up. "You check your closet?"

"Sure."

Rainey felt Safari's tense demeanor, and not wanting the drama, she dipped into the living room. "You want something to drink…some wine?" She turned toward her bag, I bought some more of that stuff you like…*Chardonnay*."

"No, I'm alright." She sat down. "Look…we need to talk."

Rainey poured a drink and faced her. "Can it wait? I'm expecting some company. Wanted to change…take a shower, ya know?"

"Oh, so, you're going out?"

"I'll see when my friend arrives."

"Marcus?"

Rainey took a sip. "Yeah…Marcus!"

Rainey sat down close to her and noticed Safari was wearing a robe and a red lingerie top.

'*Lingerie*?' Rainey thought then glanced upstairs. "A man…upstairs, you got company?"

Safari didn't answer, instead, she got up and walked towards the steps going upstairs leaving Rainey watching. She dipped into her room telling Zeus. "Damn, this bitch stole something from me, and she acts like she's…fucking innocent!"

"Like what?" Zeus asked.

"Like something that's worth a lot of money."

Zeus walked out of the bathroom. "Shit, ask her."

"I'm not one hundred percent sure."

Zeus walked over to her. "Look, you know. Whatever it is, confront her. Trust me, you'll feel a whole lot better." He turned around picking up his clothes. "Does she know we're leaving…you gonna tell her?"

"No!"

Zeus turned. "No, hold up, Safari. I can tell by the way you just answered, somethings up. What did she steal?"

Safari sighed. "My corporate folders with my Article papers and Governance papers."

"What…seriously…why! Yeah, you need to confront her."

Safari shook her head. "Stay here, I'll be back."

"Remember now, we need to go."

Safari walked out of the door, and Rainey had already dipped into her room. She walked to the door and started to knock, but then changed her mind and barged in. "Rainey, where is it!"

Rainey was on her knees searching for something underneath her bed. Safari had never tripped over a pair of shoes before, much less her borrowing clothes, shoes, or even money. Then slowly it dawned on Rainey.

"She must realize the file is missing?" she said to herself. She had to play it off to find out more. "What are you talking about. I told you I don't have the shoes…"

"No, the fucking file. Where's it at?"

Hovering over her now. Safari snatched back the covers on her bed. "Where's it at?"

"What are you talking about, Safari?" Rainey stood up now. She was half-ass livid from the encounter. "Are you fucking serious?" She mugged her and backed up some. She wasn't about to fuck up her scheme now. "Get the fuck outta here!"

Safari brushed past her into her closet tossing everything around. "Where is it!"

Rainey walked over to the closet. "What the hell are you doing, Safari?"

Safari turned around toward her. "Where's the fucking file?"

Rainey just froze.

"Is this what our friendship has reduced us too?"

"Safari…I…I…"

"I what…I did everything for you. Paid everything for you to have a good life! Stealing from me…that's some sneaky ass shit!"

Faced off like strangers it was clearly snowballing into something much bigger than nitpicking over clothes.

Rainey stood her ground. "Safari…what are you saying?" She extended her arms to embrace her. "We need to talk…"

Collapsing against the doorway of the closet, Safari burst into tears, sobbing and her knees buckled. "It's that guy, right, Marcus?"

"I don't know what you're talking about…"

"Yes you do, I know what's up!"

At the sound of his name, she knew Safari knew definitely something was up. So, she decided to manipulate the conversation in hopes of finding out more of what she knew.

"Did he tell you to steal the files…for, Gunzz?"

"No…"

"What does he want…more money?"

'*Fuck it*,' Rainey thought, she owed her at least something. "Your company."

"My company, why?"

Rainey sighed. "Safari…damn girl. You're worth millions damn near, and you're on some old philanthropy bullshit. He approached me, offered me money. I cut to the chase and got straight to business. He wants more than a seat, though," she said flippantly. "You built a corporation from the debt your father owed."

"I paid him back! So, what's his aim?"

Rainey bent down, reached underneath her bed and started pulling out a bag. "I'm not sure."

Safari walked past her. "You need to give me back my shit. If you don't, I'm going to the police."

Inside the bag was a gun that Marcus had given her. She reached in for it. "I wouldn't do that, Safari."

Safari paid her no mind and slammed the door on her way out. Rainey took out the gun and checked the .38 to see if it was loaded, it was.

"I'ma have to kill her," she mumbled quietly. She sat down on the edge of the bed with her head hung down. Then a tear fell from her eyes. Damn!"

LOVIN' SAFARI

CHAPTER 13

Marcus put the gun he had into his jacket pocket along with his cellphone and got out the car. He looked up and down the street cautiously. Then closed the door making sure it wasn't locked. He left a key in the ignition so when he came back, he could just crank up and go quick. He put on a pair of shades, and a hat tipped close toward his face with his jacket collar up looking inconspicuously. He hugged the curbside and walked swiftly up the street. He dipped into the alleyway he'd checked out earlier.

He stopped and peeked into the garage, searching for any movement. Finding none he kept it moving towards the back looking for an opening. He hugged the side of the wall, pulled out his cell phone, and dialed Rainey getting no answer. Rainey still had her head down whimpering, thinking about how she was going to muster up the nerve to even hurt Safari, much less kill her.

'Maybe I can scare her into not calling the cops,' she thought.

She had another plan and didn't need that type of drama. But right now, it seemed as if nothing would pan out. The other individual involved in her scheme she hadn't heard from, yet. She took a deep breath trying to compose herself.

"Okay," she said, her phone was downstairs, and she needed to make a call.

She stuffed the gun into an overnight bag along with the files and started for the door. Then, she stopped and looked down. She kicked off her heels, rushed into the closet, and spotted a pair of tennis shoes. She knew she would need them because she was going to have to dip out of the door fast. She peeked out and glanced downstairs. Her clutch bag was on the couch. She then glanced over at Safari's room door, and it was cracked some. She could hear voices, someone else was in there with her, a man.

"Fuck it, rush downstairs," Rainey coached herself. "I'll tell her I'm going to a hotel, and I'll be back later and we can talk then." Some old bullshit she figured, but she had to do something fast. Time wasn't on her side. She burst through the door and rushed towards the stairs.

Halfway down she heard Safari open her door and yell. "*Where the fuck you going? Oh, hell no!*"

Rainey kept moving into the living room. She grabbed her bag and started towards the door. Then she looked up and saw a man rush out charging down the stairs.

"Hey, don't go out that muthafuckin' door!" It was Zeus.

She reached the doorknob and he was down the stairs already. He was close up on her and was about to pounce when out of nowhere the door to the garage opened and Marcus jumped out.

"*Stop…Zeus…stop where you are, now!*" Marcus yelled. "*And put your hands up…high!*"

Zeus recognized the voice and stopped dead in his tracks. Knowing Marcus, he had a gun. Zeus put up his hands and slowly turned around.

"I knew you'd be coming," Zeus said.

"Yeah…you knew. Actually, I'm surprised you're still here," Marcus replied.

Safari rushed out of her room and looked down at them. "*What the fuck is going on!*" she yelled.

Marcus looked upstairs then at Zeus and snickered. "Pussy huh? You're slippin' dude."

"Well, I'm tired of you and Gunzz's bullshit…"

"Look, let's make this easy. We can go get the money you owe, Gunzz. I'll kill the girl, then maybe I can look the other way. You can go somewhere far. I don't know…maybe Alaska or something."

Zeus just shook his head. "I wish it was that easy."

Marcus turned his attention to Rainey. "You got the files, right?" Rainey picked up the bag and nodded. "Okay then, bring it over to me." She shook her head. "C'mon girl, stop the bullshit!" She shook her head again, and Marcus spazzed on her. "*Stop playing goddamn games!*"

Marcus didn't notice Zeus as he got close up on him. He grabbed his arm, then kicked his leg out from under him. Marcus tumbled forward and tried to straighten himself up. Zeus followed through with a hook to his chin. Marcus sprawled backward and the gun fell out of his hands onto the floor.

"You want to do it this way?" Zeus said as he rolled up his sleeves.

Marcus snarled, then reached into his jacket and pulled out a knife. "Yeah…okay, I'll cut your throat first and when you're dying, then I'll blow your brains out!"

Zeus put up his hands. "Sounds like a plan then."

Rainey looked back upstairs and noticed Safari had disappeared from view. She gathered her bearings and realized that somehow during the scuffle she was now in between them and the door. She fell back against the wall with the bag held tightly to her chest. She reached into her bag and searched for her cellphone, it wasn't there. She glanced over by the couch and realized she'd dropped it.

"Damn!" her mind screamed. She had to get out of the door.

Zeus and Marcus exchanged blows. They fought hard with Zeus getting the better of him. Marcus had managed to land a few and even sliced across Zeus' chest and arms with the sharp six-inch blade. But Zeus wasn't slowed. Marcus knew he didn't have any wins, so he was going to have to go for the gun. He swung the knife at him, then lunged making Zeus dip to the side. He rolled and jumped on the gun. Zeus was right on him. They both grabbed it and rolled some more struggling until Marcus was on top of Zeus with the gun to his chest.

Then suddenly two shots rang out. Pop! Pop!

They both looked at each other stunned. Marcus snarled again, then rolled off of Zeus. He had two holes in his chest with smoke coming out of the small holes.

Zeus Jumped to his feet looking down at him. "Damn, man…why? We were friends!"

Marcus' eyes rolled around in his head, and he managed to focus on Zeus. "We still are…I just wanted to be…you…" Then his head fell backward, and he was dead.

Zeus shook his head, then called up to Safari. "Safari, let's go! We gotta move!"

"I'm coming, get the bag from, Rainey!"

Zeus glanced her way and she started to run towards the door. He grabbed at her, then the front door burst open, and standing there was Gunzz.

Zeus backed up, Rainey ran over to him and gave him the files. "Damn…it's about time you got here!"

****

Gunzz stepped through and glanced at Marcus' body over on the floor. He looked up at Zeus. "You killed your

104

buddy, huh?"

Zeus nodded. "Yeah…hopefully…you'll be next." Zeus stared at him, waiting for a move.

When it came, it wasn't from him, Safari screamed out. "Rainey, don't give him the files…please!"

Gunzz reached into his pocket, pulled out a gun, and pointed it at Zeus. "Step back, Zeus, don't make a move!"

He started easing back toward the door, and Rainey reached for the doorknob to open it.

Safari yelled at her. "Rainey, think about what you're doing. Whatever deal you got going with him, he's going to renege on it. Trust me, he ain't shit…he killed my father!"

"Yes, I did, and…you were next!"

"But why? I gave you what you wanted!" She eased back towards her room. "We could have worked something out with the corporation if that's what you wanted."

"Share…" Gunzz shook his head. "No, it's too late for that now." He lifted up the files. "It's all mine now!"

Rainey turned and looked her way. "Sorry, Safari, but you wouldn't listen."

"You wasn't talking about nothing!"

"Was I not? All those years I stood in your shadow while you shined. Like I was your fucking sidekick or something."

Zeus charged at Gunzz. and knocked him down to the floor. The gun flew out of his hands. Gunzz wrestled with him as he tried to reach for the gun. Gunzz pulled at him punching him in the kidney. Rainey reached into her clutch bag for her gun.

Safari raced into the room and grabbed the .9mm she had, cocked it, and that's when she heard a gunshot. She raced back out and saw Zeus clutching at his chest as Gunzz pushed him up off of him.

"Noooo!" She took aim, but shots rang out again. She ducked behind the banister and peeked up. Rainey was shooting at her. "Rainey, why are you trying to kill me?"

Gunzz answered as he got to his feet. "Because in all of this…she's my fucking partner. It was never about that clown Marcus. Hell, she just set him up to do the dirty work."

Safari looked over at Rainey. "That's right, Safari. I brought Gunzz in. And, I also arranged for the same muthafucka you fell in love with…to kill you."

Safari shook her head, she couldn't believe Rainey was this dirty. All these years, but there was also something she never shared too. She stood up, took aim and fired off three rounds at her. Rainey dived to the floor and shot back.

Safari was well trained in ammunition and weapons. Her father's friends that had seats on the Board made sure of it because they had a premonition that she would someday, need it. They knew Gunzz would never let her old man rest in peace. She stood again and littered the wall above their heads with slugs.

"Trust me…I'm being generous. Now, throw the files on the floor."

Rainey counted shots and she only had two more rounds. She peeked over at Gunzz and pointed to the door. He nodded. Safari eased over towards the stairway with her gun still pointed at them. When she approached the top step, Rainey stood up and fired. Safari ducked, and that's when Gunzz opened the door and scrambled through. Rainey was right on his heels.

Safari ran down the steps and bolted to the door, but they had already dived into the car. Gunzz's driver stepped on the gas and they hauled ass up in the street. Safari ran out into the streets with her gun pointed, she could see Rainey as she peeked out the back window, laughing.

Safari mouthed the words. "I'm gonna get you, bitch!"

She heard Zeus groaning from inside and ran back in. He was stretched out on the floor struggling to get up.

She rushed over to his side. "Zeus…don't move. I'm gonna get you to a hospital."

He leaned up and said to her, "No, I'll be alright. You need to haul ass."

"No, I can't leave you."

"You got to, I'll be alright…"

A tear came from out the corner of her eyes. She rubbed at his face, feeling his scar. "Thank you, Zeus…"

"You knew, huh?"

"Yes…"

"I'm so sorry, I was young, I didn't know…"

"Shhhh, I forgive you!"

"Gunzz…he'll never let up. Don't let him know where you're going…"

"I got him, don't worry."

Safari and Zeus could hear the sounds of Police sirens in the background getting closer.

"Go Safari, go!" he said.

She leaned into him and kissed him on the lips. "I love you!"

"I love you, too…now go!"

She got up, ran upstairs and grabbed her bag. Then sprinted back down the stairs, glanced over at Zeus as he waved her on.

"Hurry up, Safari!" Dipping into the garage she hurried toward the back and grabbed at the tarp that covered the Ducati 1098s. She put her helmet on and got on the high-powered motorcycle. She secured her bags around her and thrust the bike toward the front of the garage. She pressed the garage door button, waited for it to open, then she cranked up. She could see the flashing lights of the police cars about a block or so away. She turned the opposite way, glanced back at the condo once more and hauled ass, vowing revenge, on Rainey…and Gunzz.

CHAPTER 14

Zeus woke up in Des Peres Hospital a week later, handcuffed to the bed. The first thing he saw was the blinking of the heart monitor overhead, as his mind drifted into consciousness.

He didn't remember too much after Safari left, but he'd heard the bike roar away from the condo. When he tried to get up, he collapsed onto the floor. He then turned over on his stomach and tried crawling toward the back door, thinking maybe he could stand himself up and possibly make it to his car. But he'd lost a lot of blood and was too weak.

The cops busted through the door with guns drawn. "Freeze, don't move!" they yelled.

They were all over the place, it seemed like there were hundreds of them, that's about the time when he passed out. Now, here he was in a bright hospital room with monitors all up in his face. He tried to lean up, and it was as if a ton of weight was sitting on his chest. He peeked down and saw gauze wrapped around his chest. He gasped, that caused his lungs to rise in his chest, it made his ribs hurt like all hell, and he hollered out. "Awww, damn!"

Then, he remembered the gunshot wound to his chest from Gunzz. Now, he was more pissed than hurt. But he was glad he was still alive. Now, he was going to make sure he didn't make the same mistake Gunzz had, by letting him live. He strained his arms underneath him to support him, so he could at least lean up a little. That's when he saw the uniformed officer staring in the face. "You okay, you want a nurse or something?"

Zeus squinted his eyes to get a better view of him. The sun shone bright through the window. "Yeah…sure," he said.

The officer got up, stepped to the door, opened it slightly, and waved his hand. A few minutes later, the Nurse was there asking what he needed. Zeus just wanted to get cleaned up and ask her the extent of his injuries. She told him she'd work on the clean part, but the Doctor would be the only one to answer the latter. He understood. The officer asked again if he needed anything. Zeus just shook his head. He was content with the juice the nurse brought in, at least until later. He laid back down and went to sleep.

Later on, when he awoke, he leaned up and noticed a different Officer was there. Then, he glanced over to the window and noticed the sun was just coming up. He must have slept until the next day. He asked the Officer what day it was, and he was right. They must have changed shifts too. He laid there and waited for chow to come.

After eating something he couldn't quite figure out. A mixture of proteins and what looked to him to be oats. He waited on the nurse to come and wash him, and subsequently change his bedpan. He hated it, but he knew it was part of the healing process. Until he gained some strength, he had to allow her to do her job, and he did just that.

He felt cleaner afterward and was able to lean up on his own a little. The cuffs on his arm restrained his hand, but they weren't too tight. But still, he couldn't help but wonder what he was being charged with. He didn't bother to ask the officer, because he knew eventually someone was going to come see him, especially once they knew he was awake.

That time came without hesitation, he was awakened again by the sound of footsteps entering his room. He opened his eyes and looked up. Four people, some older white guy in a white hospital coat, and a clipboard, more than likely the Doctor. Then, two men in suits, one was white and short, the other one was one black, tall and slim. Just by the looks of them, he could tell immediately that they were Detectives. Right behind them both was a female. She was light-skinned and very pretty.

She stepped in between them and smiled. "Hello, Zeus."

"Tabitha…" Goddamned Tabitha, he sighed. He hadn't seen her in a minute. He wondered at first why she was there, then it dawned on him that she worked at St. Louis County Prosecuting Attorney's Office. He nodded and asked, "What's going on?" He shook the cuffs on his hand.

The Doctor stepped closer. "One minute, Mr. Beloit, let me check you out first."

"Okay, Doc…what's going on with it…the wound?"

"Well…" He lifted up the gauze and poked around, causing Zeus to cringe a little. "…gunshot wound was pretty serious."

"I know that. How serious?"

"Actually…" he said as he stepped back after taking the stethoscope from off his chest. "…not as bad as it could have been. You're in good shape, so you'll heal pretty quickly. The bullet went in and hit a rib…actually three. Fractured one and broke two before ricocheting off to the right and exiting."

"Wow!"

"Yeah…lucky, but still the ribs just about punctured your lung. Matter of fact if it wasn't for the bullet hitting the rib, it would have gone straight through your heart."

"Ouch!" He grimaced as he tried to lean forward.

"Just be cool, rest a while. You'll get stronger." The Doctor turned towards the Detectives and Attorney. "Okay, that's it for me, he's all yours." He turned back towards Zeus as he was leaving out. "I'll see you later on in the week."

Zeus smiled and nodded. He thought about waving back but glanced over at the cuffs, then the Detectives. "What am I being charged with?"

The Detectives looked over at each other, hunched their shoulders, then looked back at the Officer. "Hey, what's with the cuffs?"

The Officer looked back at them. "He came in with them. Hell, they kept them on, and then had us coming back and forth in shifts to watch him That's all I know."

The Detectives gazed at each other dumbfoundedly, and then the white one spoke up. "Then, who the hell authorized this? Goddamn, what kind of shit is…"

Tabitha stepped forwards. "I did, it was my office, upon my orders."

"But…uh, why?"

"Well, we know, Mr. Beloit. We know who he knows, and even somewhat have an idea of his…profession." She glanced over at Zeus. "Trust me, we didn't want, Mr. Zeus Beloit here to leave before we got a chance to ask him some questions." She got closer towards Zeus. "And hopefully…we'll get answers. Right, Mr. Zeus Beloit?"

Zeus looked up at her and sighed. "Sure…whatever you say."

Tabitha had the Officer undo Zeus' cuffs. "Is that better?" she asked.

Zeus rubbed his wrist. "It is but…" He looked up at her side-eyed. "What do I have to do now?"

Tabitha turned towards the Detectives and told them to leave. Right after she made a call on her cellphone to Police headquarters and had them pull back their Officers.

Once that was done, she directed her attention back to Zeus. "I need some information."

"*Information?*"

"Yeah, tell me a little bit about, Gunzz's contacts…maybe." Tabitha smiled, then moved closer towards the bed. "Is it…a problem?" she said as she reached over and pulled back the covers, then stuck her hand underneath feeling on his strong, but now gauzed-up chest. She asked him. "It hurt?"

Zeus grimaced some, then said, "Look, I don't think we need to be doing this." She started sliding her hand down into his boxers. "Someone may come in," Zeus protested.

She peeked back at the door. "You know…you might be right."

Pulling her hand back, she walked over to the door and locked it. "I guess we won't have that problem now." She started unbuttoning her blouse and Zeus was taken aback at her chest. It was so full and plump. The purple lingerie she wore was lace and had a cleavage cut to die for, that pushed up the bouncing titties up. The chocolate-brown areola of her nipples in contrast to her light complexion kept his eyes peeled on her.

"Tabitha…come on now. What we had was years ago. It was fun then but were adults now. We don't have to do these things."

"Always the gentleman," she purred.

She reached back, unhooked her bra and tossed it at him. It landed in front of him, her titties bounced unmercifully in front of him as she walked closer toward the bed. "Remember these?"

All Zeus could do was shake his head. She got closer and he put up his hand. "Stop, you're trying to play me now. And you know I don't do that very well," she reminded.

"I remember. What is it you want?"

She grabbed his hand and put it on a tittie. "Like I said…Gunzz."

"What about him?"

"If you turn State, then we can give you immunity and then…"

"I'd be a rat!"

"You'd be free."

"Huh."

"Right now, Zeus. We can indict you on more than just a few murders."

"How? You'd have to prove it."

"You don't think, Gunzz kept a record of everything he paid you for. Believe me, bodyguard services don't pay hundreds of thousands."

Zeus smirked, then moved his hand away. "I hear you, but you'd still have to prove it."

She reached back underneath the cover again. Zeus tried to push her hand away, but she forced it down his boxers. She grabbed ahold of his dick and started stroking it. Zeus tried stopping her.

"I'm sure if we put your sweetheart that we've seen you with. The sweetheart that we have with you on film. The sweetheart that we can get someone to testify that she was with you on the day of the shooting. The day that Marcus was murdered…"

Zeus sighed. "Damn! Okay, what do you want me to do?"

She pulled back the cover, pulled his dick from his shorts and continued stroking. "Right, now…just relax." She got closer, then when it was hard enough for her, she bent over and gulped it into her mouth.

The back of Zeus' head pressed hard against his pillow. She sat down on the portion of the bed where his ankles were, making him vulnerable to whatever she wanted to do. He was hard pressed to move his ribs ached every time he did.

She came up off the tip of his dick and said. "I'm not the same little girl I was back in the day, huh?"

She spit on the tip, gulped it into her mouth and started sucking it deeper into her throat. She gazed up into the slits of Zeus' eyes and took a deep breath. Then ran her tongue down his shaft all the way to his balls. She licked them, Zeus squirmed, his toes curled, and she chuckled.

He looked down at her and their eyes locked. Zeus clasped the back of her head and guided her mouth back onto his dick. Hungrily she sucked up and down, and Zeus gripped the bed rails tightly.

"Ummm," she hissed sliding her lips back and forth down the length of his dick, literally face fucking her.

The warm taste of his pre-cum excited her more. She continued to bear down harder until the tip of his dick hit the back of her throat. She felt it swell up in her mouth and he couldn't hold back much longer.

He gripped her head hard with both hands, his hips rose up off the bed and the cum spewed out into her mouth and leaked out of the sides of her lips.

"Hmmm!" she cried out as she swallowed it down.

Exhausted, he fell back and just laid there. She got up off of him, reached for some tissue and wiped her lips. What she couldn't swallow, dripped out onto the side of his now becoming limp dick.

"I got it," she said as she wiped his dick off, then put it back into his boxers and pulled the covers up. She kissed him on the cheeks. "Now, rest and think about what I just said."

She got up off his bed, put her bra and blouse back on, then stepped into the bathroom to straighten herself up. When she came back out, it was as if nothing had happened.

"My people won't be back anymore. But don't go nowhere unless you let me know exactly where you're going. You hear?"

Zeus looked over at her and bit his lip. She was using Safari against him. He had no choice but to play by her rules, at least until he made some of his own. "No…problem." He said as he turned his head away.

"Good!" She unlocked the door, opened it and was out.

Zeus would have never believed what had just happened if it wasn't for the fact that his dick was still leaking cum.

CHAPTER 15

Gunzz lived in an estate over on the upscale Frontenac section or St. Louis. He was rubbing elbows with the wealthy; some legit most not. The commonality was money and lots of it. In and out all day were different people: lawyers, investors, and a whole lot of thugs and gangsters. His people on the street were the blunt of where his money came from. He may have cleaned up his act on the outside, but inside he was still dirty as hell.

He sat by the side of his full-length pool, smoking a blunt contemplating his next move. A board meeting where he would solidify his position as CEO of Wildlife Import/Export.

"Yeah." He nodded as he blew the smoke up in the air watching the white hazed vapors squandered in the wind. "It's all coming together."

Now, he could easily launder thousands and take advantage of the lucrative opiate market coming in from China that he wanted to delve into, millions could be made, easily. He finished the blunt and let in smolder out in an ashtray and got sort of a twang for something to eat. His munchies had kicked in quickly fucking with that high dollar loud.

"Rainey…Rainey!" he called out.

Rainey was in the kitchen putting together a meal of her own. "Yeah!" she answered.

"Hey, uh…could you make me a sandwich or something, and bring it to me?"

Rainey battered her eyes. "*Make you a meal*…what…where's the maid?"

Gunzz shook his head and leaned up. "Goddamn, you can't make me a fucking sandwich?"

"I can, but I'm not the maid. Isn't that the maid's job…"

"You're in the damn kitchen!"

Rainey just blew and spit in a sarcastic tone. "Okay, but, not right now…"

Gunzz was already inside when he yelled at her. "You're not doing a fucking thing!"

"I'm making myself something to eat. When I'm finished…"

"*Eat…eat…eat*, that's all you fucking do! Eat, and spend money…*my money*."

She walked toward him. "Gunzz, remember, I put in work. Those files cost me a lot."

"Oh, so that's where you're going, huh?"

"No…I'm just saying, I'm not the maid. I'm your partner!"

"A *partner* I can do…without," he said as he eased closer toward her.

"Baby…what's going on, sweetheart?" She rubbed his chest, then her hand proceeded to his dick. "You need to relax."

He pushed her away. "That's all you can do, huh…relax me? Hell, all I want is a fucking sandwich." He pushed past her, went to the refrigerator and yanked open the door. "Hell, I can always get relaxed."

Rainey just stared. "I didn't mean anything."

But it wasn't enough, she'd said too already. He was already feeling some sort of way. He slammed the food down onto the counter. "I can pay any cheap trick to suck my dick…lick my nuts. Hell…" He looked her up and down. "…and get way better pussy than what you're working with!" He laughed. "Goddamn, Marcus must have stretched the hell out of that muthafucka." He snickered.

Pissed off, she shoved her food toward him and said, "What? Okay…okay, yeah, that muthafucka fucked me good. I miss that long ass dick." She was about to walk away, then said under her breath, but loud enough for him to hear. "Better than that little ass muthafucka you workin' with."

"What!" He charged up behind her and grabbed her by the hair. "Little dick, huh?"

"Gunzz…get off of me!"

He grabbed her arms and manhandled her over to the counter. Then he slammed her down face first. "Little dick, huh, I'll show you a little dick!" He snatched her panties off and kicked her legs open. Then he pulled down his pants with the other hand and pulled out his dick. "You goddamn, bitch! This what you want, huh?"

"Gunzz…nooooo!"

He stroked his dick, it was already rock hard. He was getting off on the abuse. He spit on his hand and stroked it wet, then put it up to her ass and started pushing. Rainey struggled, but it was useless, Gunzz was much too strong for her. He pushed the head of his dick up to her asshole and started to ram it in. Rainey squeezed tightly trying to stop it, but Gunzz punched her in the back of the head causing her to smash her face into the counter.

Blood spurted out of her nose. "Muthafucka!" she screamed.

"Yeah, that's what I am." He pushed the hard dick up into her and started pumping voraciously. He looked down and could see bits of blood leaking out as he did, it excited him, and he stroked harder. "This my goddamned ass now, bought and paid for." He laughed. "Just like the rest of my whores."

Rainey just let loose and let him do what he wanted. He was right, regardless of all, she'd done for him. She was just another whore on his payroll. She thought about Safari and the double cross she pulled on her and knew she had fucked up. She was wrong for what she'd done, but most of all she was tired of being treated like a two-bit slut, fucked over by a two-bit thug.

She glanced up and saw the knife she was using earlier, but so did Gunzz. "Don't even think about it," he said.

His dick seemed to swell up inside of her stretching her asshole open mercilessly the more he fucked. She cried but it only made him fuck her harder. She could feel it as the precum leaked into her then, he exploded. Cum squirted into her bowels, and when he started pulling out, he held onto his dick, and it squirted out all over her back. All into her hair, and even the food she was preparing. He now held his limp dick in his hand as it continued to leak onto the floor. Breathing hard, he had a sick grin on his face.

It was then that the maid had walked into the kitchen. She stood there shocked, motionless. Rainey looked up in her face as she stared down at her. Tears started welling up in her eyes as the maid turned and started to walk away.

Gunzz hollered out to her. "Don't worry…" he said as he rubbed the head of his dick on her ass. "…take the day off, she can clean this shit up!" He pointed at Rainey, pulled up his pants and walked off. "And, when you're fucking finished. Make that goddamn sandwich I asked for."

Rainey sobbed and wiped at her eyes trying to get herself together. She looked at him as he walked off vowing that this would have to end, but how? It wasn't like it was the first time he'd violated her. But for damn sure if she didn't do something about it quickly, it wouldn't be the last either. Or, he might fuck around and kill her.

****

Zeus stretched out his arms in a half ass attempt to exercise them and regain some strength. He then pulled up at the hospital bed rail and leaned as far forward as he could. It hurt, but he continued stretching until he was somewhat comfortable with the pain. Fluffing up his pillows after he was finished, he leaned over and reached for the phone. He needed to make an important call.

Tired of being under Tabitha's thumb, and her watching him. Having her people come by and peep in unexpectedly to see how he was doing. What she was really doing was waiting for someone to come at him. That someone being Gunzz. He wasn't crazy though, he wasn't about to wait on that moment to happen. He needed to find a safe place, and as he reached over for the phone. He knew exactly who to call.

"Hello?"

"Zeus, oh my god! How are you? Where're you at? We've been looking for you all over the place? We heard you were dead? How come…"

"Whoa…whoa sis." He laughed. "Too much at one time. I'm okay."

"You laughing, but I told you to leave St. Louis. It's crazy there."

Zeus nodded his head. "You're right, I need to take care of some things, and who knows."

"Who knows my ass. You better bring your behind here. Don't let me have to come get you."

He laughed again. "Okay, okay, like I said. I need to take care of some things."

"Alright, Zeus, I love you."

"I love you, too, sis."

"Be careful, I suppose you want to speak to Thomi."

"Yeah. Is he there?"

"Hold on."

He could hear as she called out to him. It sounded as if he was outside. Probably messing around with the kids. He liked his brother in law. He was a good fit for his sister. He took care of the family, and Zeus was real cool with that. They didn't want for nothing. He heard footsteps coming to the phone.

"Zeus, what's up, man. Where're you at?"

He was also a good ass cop with ties in St. Louis. "Hey what's happening, Thomi. I'm alright."

"I heard about what happened. Got shot up too, huh?"

"Yeah, caught one in the chest."

"Damn, that dude Gunzz ain't shit. Been told you about him, but you knew that anyway."

"Yeah…yeah."

"And, your buddy, Marcus…now that's fucked up."

"I didn't see that one coming."

"What can I do for you?"

"Well, for one, I'm stuck here in Des Peres Hospital like a sitting duck."

"Gunzz sent anyone at you yet?"

"Naw, but I expect soon he will."

"Want me to come get you?"

"No, stay there with the family. I don't want to put you in this mix."

"I'm already in the mix…we family."

"I know…I know, but I need you there. Now, what I really need is a safe house I can go to."

"Hmmm…safe house, that can be arranged."

"How soon?"

"Hell, just say the word, I'm on it."

"Today?"

"Today it is, stay by the phone. I'll call you back in a few."

"Cool."

Zeus hung up the phone and laid down, feeling a little better. It was a healing process his body was going through. The bullet had exited his body so there were no infections to deal with. Just a broken rib and he could deal with that. The Doctor had bandaged him up pretty well, and the last time they talked he told him he was doing pretty good.

He asked if Zeus had anywhere to go instead of being there, and Zeus told him, yes. The Doctor then told him that he could release him soon. He wanted to ask why not then, but he knew why Tabitha. He knew the Doctor had to clear it first with the St. Louis County Prosecuting Attorney's Office.

He had already figured out Tabitha's little scheme. Get at Gunzz through him. Zeus snickered. Hell, when he gets at Gunzz' Tabitha should hope she's not around.

He pressed the nurse's button and she peeked her head in. "Yes, sir."

"Do you know if I had any clothes with me when I came in?"

She stepped in, went over to the closet, and looked in. There weren't any there. "No sir, but I can see what happened to them."

"No, no." He waved his hand at her. "That's okay."

She stood there after a while and Zeus looked at her curiously. He was sure hoping she wouldn't do a Tabitha on him, she had drained him enough.

She asked. "Do you need me to shave you?" She pointed around his face.

He smiled and felt at his face. He was damn sure scraggly. "You have a razor or a mirror?"

"Sure, I'll be right back." She left out.

The nurse that would normally handle his cleaning he hadn't seen in a while, but he was past the bedpan stage at this time anyway. He pressed the lever down to allow the rail to drop and wriggled his feet from under the cover to the side of the bed. When he leaned forward his chest hurt some and the rib that was broke pained him, but he fought past it. He gripped the side of the bed, stepped onto the cold tile floor and got a firm footing. He started to stand, and his legs buckled.

He was about to fall when the nurse came in and caught him. "Whoa, mister, be easy."

"I just wanted to see what I could do."

She straightened him up, then allowed him to lean on her shoulder to get his footing, and he walked on his own to the bathroom.

"That's good, I was going to suggest that because they weren't doing the bedpan thing anymore. Doctor's orders."

"That's cool," he said as he made his way to the bathroom.

"Here." She gave him the razor. "I guess you won't be needing this." She laughed as she showed him the mirror.

He laughed too. "No, guess not."

He stood up in front of the mirror examining his bruised body and she peeked her head in. "Uh, there's some man that keeps coming up on this floor and hanging around your door. We asked who he was, and he just ignored us, then sort of disappeared. Want us to call security?"

Zeus said no, thanked her and told her not to worry about it. "Next time invite him in." He winked.

She stepped back out. That must have been one of Gunzz's cronies. It wasn't Tabitha's people because all he would have had to do was flip a badge. He stretched, and then soaped up his face. He needed some clothes, and it dawned on him exactly where he was going to get them.

"Yep, it's time to go."

Thomi called him back soon after. "Yo', Zeus."

"What's up, you got a spot?"

"I got you."

"Cool."

"I got my buddy coming to pick you up. He's cool."

"I trust you."

"Bout…thirty minutes, or so."

"That'll give me time to get dressed."

"Give me a call when you get right."

"I will give sis and the kids my love."

He hung up the phone and sat on the edge of the bed quietly. After a few minutes, he heard the nurse telling someone to go in. It was the guy. He got up behind the door, and soon after it open. A bearded Spanish guy peeked his head in. Zeus grabbed him and swung him inside and tossed him to the bed. As bad as it hurt, he punched him dead in the jaw. He was out.

The nurse peeked in and said, "Everything alright?" She saw the man she had invited in out cold by the side of the bed.

Zeus said, "Everything alright…by you?"

She smiled, then reached in her pocket and handed him a number, hers. "You tell me."

Zeus reached for it. "Then, I guess, we good!"

She closed the door back and Zeus took the man's clothes off and put them on. They were a little small but pretty much not a bad fit. He picked him up, lifted him onto the bed and covered him with the sheets. Peeking out the door, he glanced over at the nurse. She nodded and pointed him toward the stairway exit. Zeus dipped into it out of sight.

CHAPTER 16

Safari opened the curtains, the sun came streaming in. She squinted her eyes, twisted the handle of the blinds and dimmed them. She yawned, then stretched and glanced around at the small guest room in the apartment she was staying in. She sighed, it was cute and would have to do. This was the safest place for her to be, at least, until she formulated her plan a little better.

Right now, Gunzz had the ups. The people that made up her Board of Directors was approached by his goons and the tim was put down on all of them and their families. The paperwork he wriggled out of her, or rather that Rainey stole allowed him to have his lawyers construe it to make it seem as if she'd relinquished her shares. Now, he would have the controlling interest and that would make him the top shareholder. The existing CEO, at least as long as she stayed out the way. It was a very hostile takeover.

As it stood now, she was considered missing and dead. For right now, she needed it to stay that way. She'd gone back over to the condo one day and noticed people searching around inside. She figured they were probably looking for more documents. They were Gunzz's people in disguise as residential managers.

She still had friends, though, people she could rely on. One of those people was a friend of hers from college. She made a call and her friend directed her to come stay with her, and she did.

Right now, she peeked her head inside the room, and said, "Good morning, I hope you slept well."

"I did, thank you."

"I put together breakfast downstairs."

"Thank you."

"And, we need to talk…something happened." She closed the door and Safari called out. "Tabitha!"

Opening back up the door Tabitha stepped in. "Yeah, what's up, Boo?"

"Have you heard from Zeus?"

She smiled and licked her lips. "Uh…yes, and no."

Safari twisted her neck. "Gurlll…you didn't?"

She laughed. "Come on downstairs, we'll talk then."

"Okay." Safari could only grin as she closed the door.

Tabitha Lavenport was just a sophomore when she met her. Struggling to make ends meet, paying for books and juggling tuition. Safari sort of took her under her wing. She helped her to graduate and acquire the Criminal Justice degree she attained. She didn't ask for anything in return. Tabitha however, made a promise that if she made it, she would be forever in her debt. Safari didn't take advantage of that then, or now. It was actually Tabitha that sought her out. She was the one who warned her about Gunzz and even Zeus.

She pulled out her toothbrush and washcloth and walked into the bathroom. Looking into the mirror she noticed worry lines embedded deep on her face. The whole thing was pretty stressful. She took a deep breath and started cleaning herself up, then Zeus popped into her mind. She wondered how he was doing. She really wanted to see him and make sure he was alright.

Tabitha hollered from the kitchen. "Come on girl, food getting cold!"

She brushed her hair, then left out of the bathroom and

put on some clothes. "I'm coming!" She got into the kitchen and sat down prepared for the breakfast and conversation Tabitha promised. "So, what's going on?" Safari asked as she gulped down a cold glass of orange juice. "And, by the way, your cooking skills have gotten a whole lot better."

Tabitha laughed. "Trust me a whole lot of pots and skillets were burned up first."

They laughed, and Tabitha pushed aside the dishes and reached for an ashtray. She pulled out a cigarette, lit it up, blew smoke into the air and leaned forward on her elbows staring at Safari. "Zeus was at Des Peres Hospital. I had him locked down…"

"*Locked down?*"

"Well, I couldn't just let him up and leave, then disappear…like he always does. So, I had some people I know from Police headquarters allow me to cuff him and keep tabs on him for a minute."

"Hmmm…okay, and?"

"We had him on ice, until he came around and started asking questions…the right ones. I had no choice…"

"You let him go?"

"No, I had to uncuff him and pull back the police. I still kept an eye on him. Me, and a few investigators I knew. But the state wasn't going to authorize the money for it and mine was running thin. Well, there wasn't much more I could do."

Safari leaned back in her chair and thought. "But what about Gunzz's people? You think they'd try him…in that environment?"

"Well, obviously Zeus wasn't about to find out. He's gone."

"Gone?"

"Yeah, my people told me he slipped out yesterday. He

left something behind though, letting us know he was getting better."

"And, what was that?"

"A body!"

"*A body?*"

"Not dead, but definitely one of, Gunzz's people. We got him and we're asking questions now."

Safari got up, scooped up the dishes and Tabitha protested. "You don't have to do that."

"No, it's cool, makes me think."

Tabitha got up and helped her. "So, where are we at with Gunzz?"

"Same ole, same ole. He had letters sent out telling everyone that there's was a Board meeting this week. I guess that's when he's going to announce the takeover."

"Wow, but can he do that?"

She looked at her and asked for the dishrag. "Yeah, his high priced lawyers know what to do."

"Can you stop it?"

Safari snickered. "Oh, you better believe, I'm working on it."

"Good." Tabitha leaned on the sink. "We have enough to build a case. Extortion…Prostitution…Drug trafficking, even Murder. But Safari, to be honest, if we go down that road. I have to warn you that Zeus would also come into that mix."

Safari sighed, then stopped washing the last dish she had; and looked up at Tabitha. "We still got a few days. I'll find him and…"

"*And what?* He's still a criminal, I know you like him and all, but it is what it is."

Tabitha walked off into the dining room. She was right,

Zeus' hands were dirty. But what was she to do? Just let them take him in. She had feelings for him, and she just couldn't let it go down like that.

She hated it, but now she had to call on that favor. "Tabitha…" Safari sat at the table in front of her. "Can you do me a solid?"

Tabitha sighed. "Damn, I know what you're going to ask. I can't do it my job would be on the line…"

"I understand, but if I was to talk to him and at least see if he's changed…"

"*Changed?*" She pushed back from the table. "I just sucked his dick the other day. He's still a dog." She shook her head. "Always has been, him and that damn, Marcus."

"Hold up, you knew him from…"

"We're from the same neighborhood. Damn Fountain Avenue. I was just a young naive girl. I fell for, Zeus, after that goddamned Marcus set it up. But he was always standoffish. Liked being to himself. Kinda weird if you ask me."

"He didn't hurt you did he?"

"No, just my feelings, that's all. He treated me kind, but he just wouldn't let me get close. He was like ice, but a sexy kind of ice. And his dick…my god, that muthafucka got a big ass dick!"

"Okay, okay, spare me the details." Safari giggled. "If I could just talk to him. See where his head is at…see if he's committed to change."

"Safari, straight up. In order for St. Louis to leave him alone. He's gotta talk against, Gunzz, that simple. And, you know he ain't no snitch."

"Least let me talk to him."

"Girl." She got closer to her and clasped her hands. "I'll

give you that, I owe you that. Find him, see what he says, then get back to me." Safari reached out and hugged her.

"Thank you so much."

"But, Safari, don't be so green. These are hardened criminals. You see what Rainey did to you when they got their claws into her."

"Yeah…I did." Safari got up from the table, rushed into her room and opened up her briefcase ruffling through some things. Notes, investigator friends…anything. Now, where do I look?" she asked herself as she ran her fingers through her long hair trying to figure out where to start. His family? What friends did he have?

Then, Tabitha stuck her head in. "You might want to start with, Gunzz. You better believe he's watching him, and when he sees you. He'll pop up for sure. That's if he feels the same for you like you do him."

She was right, Zeus would definitely be casing Gunzz out. But how the hell was she going to get around, Gunzz? He'd kill her for sure. She glanced over at her phone.

'*No, it can't be that damn easy,*' she thought. But hell, it was worth a shot. She picked it up went to her contacts and looked up, *Rainey.*

CHAPTER 17

Zeus glanced out the window in paranoia looking up and down the street. The enclosed room where he was at was situated in an apartment complex over on the East side. That afforded him the opportunity to be low profile. The cops wouldn't be in the area unless something serious was going down. Even then they'd take their time. But he knew Gunzz had snitches employed. Hell, he worked for the man, he used them his damn self. He knew there had to be a bounty on his head. He knew how Gunzz worked.

He closed the curtains and turned on the small lamp. He didn't have much, but Thomi's friend provided him with some clothes. He'd also given him two weapons, as per his brother-in-law. A .40 Glock auto, and a nine-millimeter. He had a couple of clips to go with it, but he'd have to get up close to do any real damage. If he was going to get at Gunzz he'd have to know his moves. So far, he hadn't done any public appearances or been to his office. He'd have to get him where he laid his head.

More than likely, that chick Rainey would be there, too. "Fuck her," he barked. He'd take her out on g-p, after what she did to Safari. "Safari!" He sighed.

He wanted to see her so bad and explain his feelings to her. But he'd brought enough pain into her life. Why would she go for a dude like him? A criminal…like Marcus had said, he wasn't like her. Still, he couldn't get her off his mind. That couldn't be the case because he had a mission to fulfill, a very serious and dangerous one. He wouldn't want her to be involved, or, for that matter see him. Because he was about to morph back into what he was trained to be, an assassin…a killer.

The 3500 square foot house Gunzz lived in was rather extravagant and laid out on too many acres to count. He had an indoor pool, gym, and basketball court. Four bedrooms and eight bathrooms, all full. It was spacious with a guest house right out by the pool. Rainey had done some exploring but she'd never gone inside the guest house. She hadn't seen Gunzz or the maid anywhere around, so she figured she'd go touring. She walked by the poolside admiring the serpentine cobble and bright white granite built into it. A small Jacuzzi was propped up on marble right behind it. She stopped and looked at it, then smiled.

"Yeah, tonight," she said. "Some wine and a little weed will do it."

She stepped to the door, twisted the doorknob and surprisingly enough it was open. Stepping through she admired the layout. The living room and dining room sat cozily towards the back with glass overlooking the woods. The upstairs floor had a spiraling staircase that reached up to it with iron railings. White fluffed carpeting was throughout the whole bottom floor. She liked what she saw, as she walked up the steps, she heard sounds. Voices were coming from one of the rooms. More Nosey than curious, she snuck over to the door and peeked her head in. Gunnz had the maid's ass held up in his hands pounding that ass.

That bastard!' her mind screamed.

But what was she to expect? He wasn't shit, he'd told her that. She started to turn back around, then she heard her name being called out. She'd been seen.

"Rainey…" he called out as he continued fucking her. "You want to join us?" Rainey stuck up her middle finger. "Yeah, that's what we want…to fuck you. Come on!"

Rainey slammed the door and rushed toward the stairs.

Gunzz rushed out of the room behind her. "Aw, don't get upset, I'll give you this…" He held his dick up in his hand. "…little dick, later on." He laughed then walked back into the room with the maid.

Rainey shook her head. "What the hell have I got myself into?"

She had to get out, but how? She couldn't go back to Safari, not after what she'd done. She sat down on the side of the pool and dwindled her feet in the water while the echoes of Gunzz's laughter rang in her head. She had one of the bodyguards Gunzz had employed to make a weed run for her. He didn't complain after she told him to keep it between them. Flashing her titties didn't hurt either. She grabbed a bottle of Vouvray and made her way up to her room.

Hell, even if Gunzz came in to fuck her, she'd be too damn high to give a fuck. Afterward, she figured she'd go down to the Jacuzzi and soak the stink from him off of her. She heard a buzzing sound. looking around she wondered where it was coming from. The bed…her phone, who could be calling her? She picked it up, it was Safari.

She sat down and put it up to her ear. "Hello?"

"Rainey, it's me, Safari. I…"

"Hey…uh…"

"Let's talk, I need you."

"I need you too, and I'm sorry."

"You know anything about, Zeus?"

"All I know is he's angry, and he's probably coming…"

Rainey cried out again. "Oh, my God, he's coming to kill me, right?"

"Not if I can help it."

"What do I do?"

"I need to get close…inside, so Zeus can see me. I need to talk to him."

"Okay, I can do that…"

"Rainey…Rainey!" It was Gunzz calling her name. "Where are you?"

"I gotta go, call me back later."

"I will."

She slid the phone underneath the mattress and Gunzz walked through the door. "What are you doing? Who was you talking to?"

She had to think fast. She opened up her hands and showed him the weed. "To myself, I've been doing that a lot lately. No one else here to talk to," she replied snidely.

"Oh…dope, okay! Go ahead and smoke your dope…drink your wine. That pussy will be good and wet when I fuck you later."

He closed the door, she got up and went to the window to look out. "Whatever Safari's got planned it better work."

Zeus had zoomed in with his scope right into Rainey's room. He watched as she answered the phone. He also saw her hide it from Gunzz when he came through the door. Why would she hide the phone? Who was she talking to? He got up and slid back down the hill that overlooked Gunzz's property. He figured he'd come back tomorrow night and scale the wall and make his way in. That was the plan.

Safari looked across the bed trying to figure out what she was missing. Her black leather skin suit was there, a black leather shoulder holster. She glanced around on the floor and spotted her leather all-terrain, steel toe boots, and gloves. Okay, she smiled like a kid on Christmas as she opened the satchel bag and scanned inside.

"Rope, machete, hook! Okay, I'm ready."

Rainey called back and told her it would be difficult to get her in through the front door. There were too many bodyguards around. So, she had to come up with another plan. Hopefully, it would be a good one. She'd literally have to wait for Zeus to make a move and camp out around the grounds of the estate in wait.

Saturday night was the night Gunzz would be alone. No company except him, Rainey, and the bodyguards situated around the big house. Then, as the morning came in, two other bodyguards would come and handle the open areas of vast real estate. She cased the place earlier in the week, and so far, that was the only flaw she'd seen. If she saw that then she knew Zeus had to have seen it too.

The biggest question was where would he come in from? The west side, where the road was, or the east where the woods lay? She had to choose. She just hoped she'd made the right one. It was imperative: Rainey's life was at stake, and Zeus' future was also, the future with her. She sat down on the side of the bed and commenced to getting dress. The sun was setting, and it was Saturday. This was it. Halfway through she heard Tabitha come in and she called out to her.

"Yeah…I'm here. What's up, Tab!"

"Nothing, I did a little shopping. Wanted to cook something later."

"Oh, okay…"

She listened as Tabitha went into the kitchen, then finished getting dressed. She strapped on the holster and secured her gun. She reached for the bag and looked through it once again.

"Clips…clips?" She looked over on the dresser, and there they were. She snatched them up, ran over to the door and listened for Tabitha downstairs. Then climbed out the bedroom window. Once she was downstairs, she took the camouflaged foliage she had put over her bike earlier and started to wheel it toward the street.

"Where're you going Safari?" She jumped, it was Tabitha. "Uh…"

Her arms were crossed, and she stood in her way. "I know you're not going to do what I think you're going to do."

"Tabitha…"

"*Tabitha*, my ass! Don't go fucking around with, Gunzz. He's got too many men. We can work something else out."

"I got to do this. Besides, it's not, Gunzz I want!"

"I know…I know, but suppose Zeus isn't there tonight?"

She tried to push past, and Tabitha got in her way again. "I got to take that chance."

She reached out to her. "Damn, you really love that guy."

Safari looked at her. "Yeah…I do."

Tabitha grumbled. "Damn…it, okay, but, if he doesn't show up. You better get your ass out of there and if you run into any trouble…"

"I know, I know, I'll call."

Tabitha reached out and hugged her. "Good luck and be careful. I'll make some calls and have some people I know to be on point. That's so if things go bad for you…"

"Okay." She reached into her jacket and pulled out her cellphone. "I'll call, I promise."

Safari jumped on the bike, cranked it up, put her helmet on and roared off.

Tabitha stood there watching as she rode away thinking. "Damn, don't fuck up, Safari…don't. On the way back inside, she reached for her phone and made a call. "Hey, wassup, I got a situation I need you to handle."

"What is it?"

"You still undercover at Gunzz's place?"

"Yeah."

I need you to secure the girl. When I call back take her to a location for me."

"I thought you wanted her to stay. Find out about the files."

"Hell, she doesn't have them anymore."

"You want me to take her out?"

"No…somebody will be coming to get her dumb ass."

He snickered. "Yeah, I hope whoever it is, comes in through the door because the security here is deep outside tonight. I don't know, Gunzz had this crazy premonition or something. He put some other people on the perimeter."

Tabitha looked up the street, and Safari was gone. "Damn!"

Zeus stepped out the cab up the street. Thomi's homeboy had picked him up. He gave him the thumbs up, and he looked up the long winding road. He tapped the side of the car, and it drove off. He figured it to be about a mile. He adjusted his bootstraps and secured the backpack around his back. He surveyed the wooded area. He would go to the east, coming in from the back side where the pool sat, then creep into the kitchen area. He wore camouflage and figured he'd go through where the foliage was the heaviest. The area around the mansion was well lit, but still, a few dim spots would cover him. He secured his gun and reached for the silencer by his side and secured it. Stretching his legs, he took off running.

His chest hurt some, but as long as he paced, he wouldn't over exert himself. He took deep breaths and in about fifteen minutes he was right behind the home. He scanned the area as he moved from tree to tree in the shadows.

He spotted four men armed with AKs and scopes. He figured as much. He knew there had to be more up front. Normally there would only be two, at least when he checked out the place the other night, that's what he saw then.

"Okay," he said. "Two extra men, no problem." He knew he had to be fast.

He took out his binoculars and scanned the windows. Rainey was upstairs, Gunzz was sitting by the patio around the pool area smoking a cigar. The side of the building up the wall was his best bet. He pulled out his gun and twisted the silencer tightly, that's when he heard noises coming up from behind him.

The footsteps that he now heard grew louder. They were getting closer. Whoever it was, was making an attempt to not be heard, but they were doing a half ass job at it. Closer, and closer it got until whoever it was, was right on him. He sprung up, grabbed them in a yoke and put the gun upside their head.

"Wait…wait!"

He cocked his head. "What the hell?"

"It's me…Safari!"

He spun her around and looked her up and down. "Safari, what the hell are you doing here?"

She smiled. "Damn, you don't want to see me?"

He snatched her up in his arms and kissed her. "Trust me…I do. But you could have gotten yourself killed." She started laughing. "What?" She pointed to his face, then wiped along it. The black grease that she had on had marked him up. He looked at her and couldn't help but start laughing, too. Then, a light started coming their way. "Duck down!"

It scanned the wooded area and then keep on its path going past them. "What are you doing here, Safari?"

"What are you doing here?"

He sighed. "I think you know."

"Zeus…baby…I've got a better way. Just hear me out…please!"

He looked at her side-eyed. Okay…talk." He checked his watch. "But make it fast, we don't have much time. A guard will be doing a perimeter walk in a little while."

"Okay…check this out," Safari said, and pulled him off to the side out of view and started explaining her plan.

LOVIN' SAFARI

CHAPTER 18

Zeus leaned back against a tree soaking in all the heavy shit Safari had just laid on him. He sighed, then looked over at her, and put his head down.

Safari reached out to him. "Baby, that's the only way it could work…and us to be together."

He took a deep breath then looked at her and spotted a glimmer come off her hand. He glanced down and saw the ring he had given her.

He reached out, grabbed her hand and lifted it up. "You're serious, huh?"

"Yes."

"I mean that much to you?"

She got closer to him. "You do, the question is do I mean that much to you?"

Zeus half smiled and pulled her in closer to him. Then ran his fingers through her hair and kissed her lips. He tasted the sweetness on them like honey as he clasped his hands around her waist. She started to grind her hips into him. His dick started getting hard, then he kissed her on the neck.

She cooed passionately. "Zeus…I love you!"

He pushed her back some then looked over at the makeshift cover he had and pulled her over by the hand. He ran his hand between her legs feeling her pussy and started to rub it until her head drew back and she moaned softly. He gently laid her to the ground and kissed her some more, his tongue tasting the sweetness of her lips.

After laying her down he reached into the leather tights she wore and started playing with her clit. Safari wrapped her legs around his waist and slow grinded, then not being able to take it anymore she reached down and pulled out his dick. Safari got up and pulled down her tights. Zeus admired the curvaceousness of her body. The small patch of curly hair that covered her pussy, and the juicy wet red clit that budded its head through. He laid back and opened his arms up wide beckoning her in.

Safari sat on him, then reached down, grabbed his dick and slid it in her. She gasped as it slid inside of her. He grabbed the makeshift tarp and covered them. He pumped his strong muscular groin slowly and methodically into her pussy, working up a froth between her legs. She matched him his rhythm, moaning and running her hands through her hair.

She called out his name. "Zeus…oh, Zeus!"

He continued to stroke until he felt her dripping on his nuts, and his dick thrust inside of her getting harder by the minute. He was about to cum, he was trying to hold back, but she clasped her legs tightly around him.

"Come on, baby…give it to me!" Safari moaned.

Zeus couldn't take anymore, he reached up and grabbed her, then pulled her down on top of him, pushed inside of her gently and felt it. It was as if a faucet had been turned on inside of him, and cum oozed out of him.

Safari laid gently on his chest taking all that he had until he fell limp inside of her. They laid there on top of each other, Safari kissed his face, then the scar on his cheek.

"Never thought I would ever see you again," she said.

"Me neither." He cuffed her small face highlighted by the moon in his hands. "I'm so sorry for what I've done. I really need you to forgive me."

"I have, really!"

They kissed more until they heard the shots. They peeked

their head out of the cover and looked around. They were coming from the mansion.

"What's that?" Safari whispered.

Zeus got up, pulled up his pants and looked over. "Shots coming from the house." He picked up his binoculars. "Oh shit!" Then pulled out his gun and started towards that way.

Safari reached out and stopped him. "No, Zeus…my way."

"But…"

"No buts."

She straightened up her clothes and they crept closer trying to get a better view. There was indeed a gunfight going on. The guards were shooting at one of their own. They both got closer and saw that the one that was being shot at was standing in front of Rainey. She was crouched down behind him. He was doing pretty good until two others arrived upstairs with their AKs and started spraying the long .39mm Caliber steel shells at him. He grabbed Rainey and ran towards the window. He busted it open and started urging Rainey to go through, then he turned and continued shooting back.

It was Tabitha's inside man, he must have gotten made. Rainey was hesitant about making the two-story leap. He noticed that, so he got closer to her, looked out the window at the bushes below and pushed her. She fell and bounced off the bushes below but got up unscathed. He looked out the window at her and took a few more shots then turned to leap himself. He caught two rounds to the back.

He reached up at the window pane and yelled, "*Rainey…run!*" Then, he caught two more to his head, and it was over with.

Rainey looked up at him in shock and was hesitant until

she saw the other guards come to the window. One of them took aim, and she dived to the ground. The bullet just missed her. She fell down then got up and zig-zagged her way running towards the tree line, coming their way.

"Zeus, she's running this way!"

Zeus stepped out of the tree line and started shooting towards the window and they ducked back inside.

Safari ran towards Rainey. "Come on, hurry!"

It was then that Gunzz and his men rushed out the back by the pool and spotted them. He pointed up towards them and his men started shooting. Safari reached out to Rainey and pulled her to the ground. Then, she pulled out her gun and opened fire at them. Zeus gave her enough cover fire for them to get up and run toward him. Safari did just that. They were just at the tree line, then Rainey dropped in her tracks. Safari yelled at her. "*Get up*!" She reached down to help her up and felt the warm blood coming from her back. She'd been hit. "Damn, come on, girl. I got you!" It was useless, Rainey's eyes rolled around in her head as Safari kneeled down next to her. "Come on, don't do this to me."

"I can't…get up. I'm sorry, Safari…so sorry…"

"Shhhh, don't talk."

"It hurts, Safari…I can't get up."

Gunzz and his men were coming up the hill towards them getting closer, and Zeus yelled. "Come on, I'm running outta clips…pick her up!" He got closer and could see that Rainey had been hit, bad.

"Damn." Safari started crying, the tears rushed down her cheeks.

Rainey looked up at her with blood running out the sides of her mouth. "Go…I'll be alright."

"No, we can pick you up."

"Go, Safari…I love you!"

"I love you…too."

Rainey grabbed her hand and squeezed it tightly, then died. Safari hollered and started shooting wildly at Gunzz and his men. Zeus rushed towards her, then he spotted the man at the window that had already started taking aim. He pushed her down and the shot whizzed past them.

"We gotta go, there's too many of them."

"No, they killed, Rainey…fuck, Gunzz!"

"Safari…come on." He looked into her eyes and pleaded with her. "Like you said, your way…right."

That woke her out of her trance, and she got up to her feet, picked up her satchel and ran towards the woods with Zeus. She looked back at Rainey laying there, then at Gunzz, and hollered, "I'ma get you…I swear!"

Gunzz watched as his men chased behind them. He caught Safari as she looked back at him yelling, then Gunzz mouthed the words. "Not if I get at you first."

Zeus lead Safari through a path he managed to mark earlier. They finally made it to the road, and Gunzz's men were still behind them. He grabbed Safari softly by the hand, looked in her eyes and then over at the long run ahead. "Can you do this?"

Safari looked back at him. He was ready to shoot it out if need be. "As long as you're right by my side."

Zeus nodded his approval at her thoroughness and started sprinting through the woods situated on the other side of the road, then out of view.

Gunzz's men stopped, he walked over to Rainey's body. "Get rid of her. We might be getting company, soon. And oh yeah…the informant, too, Rat muthafucka!"

LOVIN' SAFARI

****

Tabitha exploded after hearing the details of what happened. "Oh, my god!" She sat down and lit up a cigarette. "They killed her…him…" She took a pull off the cigarette. "My fault, I put him in there."

"But, why?"

"We needed more information on, Gunzz."

"And, you figured Rainey might lead him to it, and my files."

She stood up and approached Safari. "I'm sorry…I didn't think…"

"You're right, you didn't think. Now, she's dead." Safari sighed and looked away from her. "Okay, okay, what do we do now?"

"Well, we get a warrant."

"A warrant?"

"For murder."

"But we don't have Rainey's body or your plant."

Tabitha sighed. "But I have you and Zeus' testimony."

"Damn that!" She turned facing her. "Then, we have to own up to the guns…Zeus, all that!" She threw her hands up in the air disgusted. "I promised him he'd be okay."

Tabitha sat down again. She thought for a while, then snapped her fingers. "Then Safari, we have to get him on his illegal business practices…racketeering…extortion…bribery. Hell, there's enough there to put him away. And, that will give the Police enough time to build more of a case. More charges."

"But will it work?"

"You tell me, I still need your people that work there, their statements."

"Okay, I'll talk to somebody." Safari sighed, picked up her phone and dialed some numbers.

She turned her back from Tabitha and spoke into the phone for a minute, then looked back at Tabitha and gave her thumbs up.

When she finished the conversation, she said to her, "We might be good, but I just spoke to someone on the Board and they tell me Gunzz just called an emergency meeting. He must be going to try and vote me out, and then vote himself in."

"And…"

"And, if he does that, then he can literally disappear, legally."

"Then, we got to stop him. When is the meeting?"

"Damn," Safari said when she looked at her watch. "In about an hour."

Tabitha got up running to her room. "Then, we need to get moving."

By the time Tabitha made her calls, and they got on the road it was about forty-five minutes later. The Police met them in front of the building.

Tabitha pulled Safari off to the side before they went in. "Will, Zeus, be here?"

"No, he's going to meet me somewhere. But you did say he could get immunity for his testimony against, Gunzz, right?"

"I give you my word."

"Okay then, let's go get him."

They gathered with the Police and rode the elevator up to Safari's floor, where her Wildlife Import/Export Corporation was at, and stormed the office.

Tabitha was out in front with the warrant she had secured. "Where's the Boardroom?"

The receptionist panicked and pointed her towards the back. Gunzz's men stood there, and the Police drew their weapons ordering them to get up against the wall. Once they were secured, Tabitha opened the Boardroom door and walked in, with Safari right behind her. Gunzz was sitting at the long table in front of the other members around him.

"Ladies…what do I owe the pleasure?" Gunzz asked.

"You're through now, Gunzz!" Safari shouted at him.

Gunzz just leaned back, smirking. "For what?" He reached for the folder in front of him. "This is my company now. Get the fuck out, or, I'll have you put out."

They were too late? The vote had already taken place. Safari looked around at the other members and they nodded their heads in agreement with him, all except one.

"Was she too late?" Was all Safari could think about.

"Now…" Gunzz stood up straightening out his suit with a smug look. "…we're in the middle of an important…meeting. Would you please excuse us?"

Tabitha stepped forward with papers in hand. "Yeah…yeah, it won't be that easy. Smart, but, not smart enough." She pulled out her phone, shoved it in his face and pressed play on the video app.

It showed Rainey with files in hand giving them to him. Rainey had also recorded videos of him doing business with known gangsters and mobsters, even political figures. That was it, Gunzz had to go down. He was now too big of a risk.

The Police stepped forward. "Cuff him."

"What?" Gunzz fussed.

"Racketeering…Extortion…Bribery."

That's when the person who didn't nod stood up. He was Safari's, inside man. "I'll testify against him. He threatened me and my family."

Tabitha looked at him and nodded, then back at Gunzz. "And, that's just to start, you're going away for a long time."

Gunzz struggled as they put the cuffs on him. "You, ain't got nothing! That video is doctored. My lawyers will eat that shit up in court!"

Safari snarled in his face as he came by her. "Later…you piece of shit."

"Piece of shit…piece of shit?" He started to fight with the cops trying to get at her. "You tell Zeus I'm going to get him. There's nowhere he can hide that I won't find him! Piece of shit…rat!"

Safari shook her head as he was led out.

Tabitha asked her. "You okay?"

"I'm alright. You heard him, right?"

"Zeus is good, I got him covered. When I need him, I'll be in touch!" She looked around. "You sure he's not around?"

Safari pulled out her phone. "No, I'm supposed to meet him." She signed some papers that were put in front of her from the Board members. Papers that put her back in control. Zeus picked up the phone, and she said, "It's done."

"Okay, then, you're on the way?"

"I'm coming."

Tabitha cut in on the conversation. "Where are you guys going?"

Safari smiled at her. "Someplace…far." She rushed out of the room. "I'll call you when I get there."

Tabitha waved at her, then said to herself. "Lucky guy…lovin' Safari!"

Safari got out of the cab at Lambert-St. Louis International Airport and rushed in. She was looking for Gate 4. She spotted Zeus, ran to him and jumped into his arms. "I'm ready!"

"Okay…let's go." He pulled out the tickets and pointed toward the gate, they were going to. "That's our flight."

"Yeah…Belize."

They walked up to the counter hand in hand and presented their tickets. After checking their bags, they were escorted onto the rampway to their flight. Zeus looked around at a few suspicious people.

Safari caught onto his moment of paranoia. "Gunzz, will be gone for a long time, don't worry."

He looked around at a few in particular faces. Some that haunted him in his sleep then turned and said to her. "It's not Gunzz I'm worried about."

EPILOGUE

The bus was cold and dank, and it reeked with the smell of piss. Gunzz was the only one on it. He wriggled uncomfortably with the belly chain and cuffs he had on. The leg irons were too tight, but that was done intentionally. He fucked up and made the mistake of propositioning a C.O. the wrong C.O. The bus pulled up to the backway of the Missouri State Penitentiary. His first stop on the twenty-five to thirty bid he pleaded to.

Rainey's body hadn't been found so far, but there were enough testimonies on the racketeering charges, and extortion to bring him down. Then, he was still looking at miscellaneous federal charges also. His lawyers couldn't do anything against the video evidence, and Zeus' testimony was going to be used as evidence in other murders. Zeus was given immunity as long as he didn't violate any more laws and stayed very, very low key. Tabitha and enough of Safari's money saw to it.

He got off the bus, and after a shakedown and clothing issuance, he was escorted to his living area. Once inside the inner facility, the dorm where he'd be staying, he said to himself, "This ain't bad, it could be worse." People that recognized him nodded his way. Without a doubt, with his connections to the criminal underworld, he knew he would be alright.

After being given his room assignment, he laid out his rack and stepped on the tier. He was immediately met with daps, gifts, and contraband. A small, wiry inmate stepped to him and put out his hand. Gunzz stepped back a little, and the others that were surrounded around him stepped forward.

"Whoa…it's me."

"Me, who?" Gunzz asked.

"Muthafucking Gutta!"

Gunzz recognized him. "Damn, Gutta, been a long time!"

"Yeah…ten years."

Gunzz invited him inside the cell and they sat. "You did the convenience store hold up a while back, I remember. I bonded you out…then you fucked up again."

"Yeah…I fucked up."

"Naw, you was just fucked up. Should have handled that sober. You know you still owe me some money."

"Uh…true." He started getting nervous.

"Naw," Gunzz laughed. "Forget about it, I'm sure we can work something out in here. So, what's up?"

"Figured I'd let you in on the haps."

"Like what?" He got up and called Gunzz, and they stepped back out onto the tier. He pointed to the officer's booth on the lower level. "Over there."

"And?"

"You see that C.O., the chick? Long hair…pretty."

Gunzz squinted, then said, "Yeah, what about her?"

"Man, that's motherfucking, Mimi's daughter, Crystal."

"Trick ass, Mimi? Okay…looks like her. What about her?"

"Man…she's a plug. Trust me, bitch'll do anything for that bread."

"Anything, okay…really?" Gunzz looked her way, caught her eye, then winked and she smiled.

"She's game tight, and trust me, she knows who you are."

"Okay…that's good to know."

"But hey, if you need anything, just let me know."

He dapped him. "I might just do that, Gutta."

Gunzz walked back inside his cell and thought about what Gutta had just said. Then he got up and leaned against the door frame checking out the C.O. They were talking about and thought to himself, *'Game right, huh?'*

"Hmmm, maybe I just might be seeing you, Zeus, and your bitch, Safari much sooner…then later." He laughed.

His laughter echoed around the small closed in dorm as the C.O.'s voice came through the loudspeaker. "Count time!"

ABOUT THE AUTHOR

The author, Dean Hamid, was born and raised in Brooklyn, New York. In his youth, he read the works of Donald Goines, Iceberg Slim, as well as Richard Wright, also throwing in the poetic banter of James Baldwin over and over while hiding these books away from his parents.

Growing up in New York City's hardcore Bushwick-Hylan Projects, his writing was not necessarily intended to glamorize the quote-unquote gangsters or even the street life. But to emphasize the presence of the drama that was involved and that surrounded around it.

In the past ten years, he's been writing articles, commentaries, short stories, and has managed to complete five novels. Given the opportunity to correspond with published authors. It's been said that his work swings towards what is described as Urban Fiction Drama, with a strong propensity toward a slick old school literary voice.

Dean Hamid works hard and tirelessly to keep his work as professional, and gritty as it can be, but yet, stay literally solid. His work successfully proves and drives home this point.

DEAN HAMID

ALSO AVAILABLE:

Cold Hard
WIND.
DEAN HAMID

LOST BOY!
DEAN HAMID

* 9 7 8 1 9 4 7 7 3 2 4 7 6 *